NO MERCY

They Call Me Stormi

A Novel

FELECIA POOLÉ

No Mercy

For inquires, contact the author.

Stormii Girl Publishing
P.O. Box 44342
Los Angeles, CA 90044

Email: Stormiigirlpublishing@gmail.com

ISBN: 978-0-9978287-1-9

Facebook: Felecia Poole
Instagram: Stormii1
Twitter: Felecia Poolé @Stormiigirl
Blog: http://stormiigirl.wordpress.com

Cover Design: TWA Solutions

Editorial and Design Services: www.529Books.com

I dedicate this book to my daughter
Caila Simone; rest in heaven my
beautiful little girl.

ACKNOWLEDGMENTS

I would like to thank God first for giving me the strength to push through my second novel. "I can do all things through Christ who strengthens me" Philippians 4:13. I would like to thank my mother, Earnestine Poolé and my father, Keelo Poolé—my two biggest fans. I want to thank the love of my life, Timothy Watson, for his continuous support and motivation. I would like to thank my oldest son, Greggory; my youngest son, Khristopher; his wife, Mary Jane; and my grandchildren, Taliyah, Caila, Cali, Trason, Trinity, Kenly, Julius, and Jayla, who are the light of my life. To my siblings who support me no matter what—Mickoyan, Michael, Anita, Veronica, and Mandrake—I say thank you. To my wonderful family and friends, I couldn't have done it without your continuous support.

Special thanks to Dr. Rosie Milligan, Adrienne Russell, Niecy Taylor, Jewell Puckett, Tina Johnson, and Treva Metoyer for always supporting me.

To my Facebook, Instagram, and Twitter fans, I thank you for reading my novels. I love hearing what you think.

No Mercy

1

I'm Not Crazy

I was released into general population after being strapped down to my bed for several days. My therapist didn't like that I had called her a bitch, and I didn't like that she wanted to analyze why I had written "no mercy" in red lipstick on the mirror. She demanded I clean the mirror, so I demanded she kiss my ass.

The crazy bitch got upset and starting pointing her finger in my face; that was her first mistake.

The second was screaming at me. She had a degree in psychology and I had a degree in streetology. She told me if I didn't clean the mirror, she'd have me locked down. Threatening me was her third mistake.

I stood quietly, contemplating my next move. I took a deep breath and reached for the tissue box. When she saw I was cleaning the mirror as she asked, her tone relaxed. We engaged in conversation, small talk for the most part. I could tell she felt like she won the battle, but the war had just begun. As soon as that bitch cracked a smile, I hit her in the nose with my elbow. She hit the floor. I grabbed her by her hair and dragged her across the floor. Her screeching voice hurt my ears, so I socked her in the mouth. She started bleeding profusely. She begged me not to hit her again. I laughed uncontrollably. Before I could hit her one more time, a team of orderlies rushed in and subdued me. I didn't know she carried a panic button.

They strapped me down. They helped her up and left the room. An hour later, she returned. She had a swollen nose and a busted lip. She was mad as hell, but I didn't care.

She walked over to me and whispered, "I'm going to make you pay for what you've done to me."

"Go fuck yourself."

She took a syringe and injected me with mind-altering drugs. That bitch was determined to break me, and I was determined not to let her. I fought the effects of the drugs as long as I could before I fell asleep.

It didn't take long for the nightmares to begin. My heart started beating rapidly. I was sweating from every part of my body. I was scared. I looked down at my legs; I saw that I was standing on the edge of a cliff. Then it happened—I closed my eyes and I jumped. Before I hit the ground, I opened my eyes and saw that I was floating in darkness.

I heard a voice say, "Welcome to hell. I'm the ruler of the darkness. I have dominion over the earth. I will help you avenge all the pain that has been inflicted upon you. Serve me and give me your soul. Together we will show your enemies no mercy."

After I told the darkness to take me, I saw a bright light. I heard a voice say, "You can do all things through Christ who strengthens you" Philippians 4:13. "Seek the kingdom of God above all else, and live righteously and he will give you everything you need" Matthew 6:33.

As the days went by, the hallucinations continued. I remained strapped down and was deprived of food and water. I hadn't bathed in days, and I could smell the stench coming through my panties.

Finally, after being kept in a comatose state, a nurse's aide came to check on me. She thought I was asleep. I could barely open my eyes, but I could see her staring at me.

"Oh my God, what have they done to you?"

She lifted my head to give me a drink of water. She used Vaseline on my dry, scaly lips to stop them from cracking. She took a wet cloth and washed my face. With the tip of her index finger, I felt her draw a cross on my forehead. She walked around my bed, praying for me.

As she proceeded to leave, I reached out to her. Despite the hand ties that had me strapped down, I was able to touch her hand. She turned and looked at me. In a low, raspy voice, I begged her for help. The pain I felt from being on my back for such a long time combined with the lack of food made me give into their methods of reprogramming. She left the room and returned with a nurse. The nurse untied me and they both helped me up.

As I sat up, I became dizzy. The ties that bound me had been too tight. The blood circulation in my hands had been decreased. My wrists were puffy and numb.

I needed them to feel like they broke me, and that their so-called treatments worked, so I acted apologetic for my actions. All the while, my intentions were to slap the dog shit out of both these bitches. But I remained calm, for fear I would jeopardize my freedom. Besides, I didn't have any feeling in my hands, and it would have been literally impossible for me to slap someone. The person that deserved an ass kicking was my therapist. I had to play it smart. I knew the day would come when I would pay that bitch back for her kindness.

Before I could get out of the bed, my catheter had to be removed. The nurse asked me to lie back and spread my legs apart. As soon as I opened my legs, the horrific smell of a pussy that hadn't been washed in days hit her hard. I wasn't even embar-rassed. They say cleanliness is next to godliness. Well, it was safe to say I was nowhere near being godly. My jewel box smelled foul. I hoped the use of soap and water would be my cure.

The nurse helped me sit on the edge of the bed with my legs hanging, not quite touching the floor. The heaviness of my legs required me to move slowly. I had to allow the blood to circulate down to my toes so I could walk. When I was able to wiggle my toes, the nurse helped me walk to the shower area. I felt weak; it was hard for me to stand. The nurse asked if I needed help cleaning myself. I shook my head and pointed to the hand-icapped shower. I needed to use the handrails to help me stand. She helped me into the shower and gave me towels, a bar of soap, and some hygiene products. She told me to push the buzzer if I needed help.

I turned the hot water on in the shower and let it run for a minute. I wanted the water to get hot, as hot as it could get. I removed my hospital gown and stepped into the shower. The pulsation and the heat on my naked body started to relieve my tension and anxiety. I stood directly under the showerhead and let the water run down my face. I washed my hair in the sweet smell of coconut and jojoba oil shampoo. I rinsed, applied conditioner, and pulled my hair back into a ponytail. I took the bar of soap and lathered up my body, paying special attention to my jewel box. I removed the showerhead from its holder and held it close to my jewel box, rinsing away the unpleasant aroma. I felt refreshed. The only thing left to do was give myself a trim. As I finished, memories of Bryce crossed my mind.

The mind-blowing experience of him teaching me how to trim my private parts—and him performing oral sex on me afterwards—was still in the forefront of my mind. Every time I needed to give myself a trim, I thought of him. He helped me move on from my heart breaking experience with James, who was my first love. Bryce was my ray of sunshine…so I thought. I had never experienced oral sex before, and Bryce made it all about me. He wanted nothing in return.

James took my pearl of innocence. At the tender young age of thirteen, I was ripe like a sweet peach and ready for the picking. I was unaware of my sexual beauty. My tall, thin frame embodied the seduction of a young woman. My small waist and thick thighs made grown men weak in the knees. James took advantage of my immaturity and led me to believe I was special to him. I ended up in a vacant house on a dirty mattress with my legs in the air.

Most men just wanted what was between my legs.

After being sexually involved with James and Bryce, I now understood the power of the pussy. It was like a magnet. It exudes a force that attracts the male. Once he enters the force field, he's rendered helpless.

The thoughts of my past made me emotional and I began to sob like a child. I bit down on my bath towel so no one would hear me. I slid down the wall of the shower and sat on the floor. With tears in my eyes and snot running down my nose, I began to think of what my life would be like if I had kept my virginity.

In my purity class, I learned that sex was for married people. It's a pleasure that God ordained for them. Maybe, if I would've kept my legs closed, I wouldn't be stripped down emotionally.

My life had become a rollercoaster ride. I was numb to doing the right thing. I just didn't care anymore, so I hooked up with Trent, another older guy that I had met at a party. He taught me how

to make money selling weed and black mollies. After several months, he professed his love for me.
He was just another lap dog. He would lick it, but
he wouldn't stick it.

I found the strength to get up off the shower
floor. As I stood up, blood began to run down my
leg. I leaned against the shower wall. I began to
have flashbacks of Derrick lying face down in a
puddle of blood.

*I saw Asia, working tirelessly to save him. She
turned him over on his back to see if he was still
breathing. He was slipping away fast. She gently
tilted his head back to blow breath into his lungs
and started chest compressions. When the paramedics arrived, they took over. They worked fe-
verishly to bring Derrick back, but they weren't
able to get his heart pumping.*

*The kiss of death was on my baby brother's
face as his limp body showed no signs of life. The
bullet lodged in his stomach was causing him to*

bleed out. His face had turned purple and his eyes had rolled back in his head.

Death called Derrick's name. He died horribly. He was shot down in the street like a dog. Once the paramedics called time on Derrick, Asia refused to give up. She jumped on top of the gurney, straddled Derrick, and began speaking in her heavenly language. She told God she had been praying long and hard; she asked for him to intervene.

Asia continued to blow breath into Derrick's lungs, and God gave him back his life. He was rushed to the hospital where emergency surgery was performed.

Derrick remained in a coma after having three major surgeries in one week. Our mother sat by his bedside day in and day out, waiting for him to wake up. She believed the God she served would heal him.

Once again, I was in the midst of the storm. After losing my best friend, Shannon, to suicide, the thought of losing Derrick was unbearable. My sanity had escaped me.

I was committed to a psychiatric hospital. I lived among people with all forms of psychosis. Reality was not a part of their world. These people became my friends. Some had been abused by their own family members. Some were products of incest and rape. Some of them were murderers. The reason for them being there didn't matter; we all shared a familiarity with some form of psychosis.

"Like minds think alike."

"If you've never ventured into your dark side, you'll never understand the genius that lies within you. People don't realize they're one step away from insanity. Some get to visit and some get to stay. The mind is a terrible thing to waste."

After my shower, I was taken back to my room and given a hot meal. I couldn't eat all my food even though I had hunger pains in my stomach. Every bite made me feel like I wanted to throw up. When the nurse came to take my plate, she asked if I wanted to go to the dayroom. I hadn't seen the sun for several days, so I was eager to go. While walking down the hall I became very tired. The nurse saw I was holding onto the wall, so she got me a wheelchair.

She pushed me over to a window so I could feel the sun on my face. I closed my eyes and suddenly felt at peace. The same peace I felt when I was with Justin.

After looking for love in all the wrong places, I had finally met someone who understood me. He came into my life at a time when I needed change. He was full of life and energy. He knew what he wanted and he was determined to get it. He was the poster child for doing the right thing. He was a track star headed to college. He helped me get back to living a normal teenage life. He treated me with respect. Instead of being concerned with my jewel box, he was concerned with my heart.

I tried to regain some form of normalcy after finding out Derrick was still alive—if you call being assisted by machines living. I thought about everything I would do once I was released. Vengeance would be mine.

My brother was in the hospital waiting for death to call his name. The rage I felt would be released on the person that shot him. I will go to my grave seeking revenge. I will show them No Mercy. I am my brother's keeper.

THEY CALL ME STORMI RAIN

2

STILL ALIVE

"**M**rs. Johnson, your son has been in a coma for several weeks with minimal brain activity. You may want to consider taking him off life support," the doctor stated.

"Doctor, I want you to listen to me, and listen good. My son is covered with the blood of Jesus. It's not over until God says it's over."

"Heavenly Father, hear my prayer. I come boldly to your throne of grace asking for mercy

for my son. Lord, this is the baby boy that you have given me. I speak life into his body in the name of Jesus. I decree and declare that his organs will function and he will be restored. I speak healing in the name of Jesus."

While my mother sat at Derrick's bedside holding his hand, in walked a detective.

"Hello, Mrs. Johnson, my name's Detective Grey. I'm working on your son's case. I have some good news. We've made an arrest. Babette Lewis was one of the prime suspects in the shooting of your son. We searched her apartment and found the gun your son was shot with."

"What? You've got to be kidding me. That crazy woman shot my son?"

"Yes, she did."

"Thank you Jesus. I knew my God would reveal the shooter."

"She's been arrested for attempted murder, but we have a problem."

"What's the problem?"

"She doesn't have any known relatives and she has a five-year-old son."

"What does that have to do with me?"

"She states that your husband is her son's father. She wanted your husband to take responsibility and allow her son to be a part of his family. When he refused, she decided the only way to get his attention was to hurt one of your sons. I was wondering if you'd consider taking her son into your home, so we don't have to put him into foster care."

"I can't believe you have the audacity to ask me to allow that woman's son into my home. There isn't any proof that my husband is his father. You must think I'm a damn fool."

"I had to ask, Mrs. Johnson. He's in need of a home and I thought you might consider taking him in."

My mother had to deal with the possibility that her husband had an illegitimate child; her son was in a coma and might die; and her crazy ass daughter had been committed to a psychiatric hospital. That was a lot to deal with. Where was her God?

The detective departed, and in walked my father. His eyes were bloodshot from drinking all night.

"How's Derrick doing?"

"He's holding his own. My God is going to restore him."

"What are the doctors saying? I didn't ask you about God."

"If you wanted to know what the doctor's had to say, you should've had your drunken ass here earlier. You should be worried about yourself; you've broken the sanctity of our marriage. Trust me, you're going to pay for it."

"What do you mean by that?"

"You'll find out. You need to sit with Derrick in case he wakes up. Stormi is being released to-day and I have to pick her up."

"Are you sure she's ready to be released? It took a year before she could get it together the first time. Don't rush her treatment just because you want her home."

"Look motherfuc—you're about to make me say something I may regret later. You need to be worried about your outside affairs and let me worry about my children. Stormi is coming home today."

THEY CALL ME STORMI RAIN

3

STORMI'S RELEASE

"Hello, my name is Mrs. Johnson. I'm here to pick up my daughter. She's being released today."

"Good afternoon, Mrs. Johnson. I'll check with the doctor to see if your daughter is ready. What's her name?"

"We call her Stormi."

"Oh, I know who you're talking about. She calls herself Stormi Rain around here."

"When did that happen?"

"You'll have to ask her doctor. I'll page her for you."

"Okay, thank you."

The doctor answered the page and instructed the nurse to send my mother to her office.

"Good afternoon, Mrs. Johnson. I'm Dr. Montgomery, Stormi Rain's primary mental health psychiatrist."

"What's with this Stormi Rain business? Why did she change her name?"

"Stormi has dealt with a lot of tragedy in her life. Instead of confronting her fears, she has chosen to remove herself from the situation. Changing her name to Stormi Rain empowers her to start over and gives her control over her life."

"Doctor, do you agree with this behavior?"

"Well, mental illness, like many other chronic illnesses, requires on-going treatment. We'll need to continue to monitor her. She's required to attend a weekly one-on-one therapy session with me. I'm sure her fascination with calling herself Stormi Rain will eventually stop."

"Should I refer to her as Stormi Rain?"

"No, refer to her as Stormi. If you accept her name change, she'll continue with it."

"Why do you refer to her as Stormi Rain?"

"She's my patient. It's a form of therapy. She feels more in control because she's in a different environment. Once she returns to her normal environment, she will revert back to being Stormi."

"If you say so. My faith is in God. I know that my God will see Stormi through this trying time. He will restore her mind."

"Yes, Mrs. Johnson, I understand. Well, Stormi is waiting for you at the nurses' station. I have signed all her release papers. Make sure she's here once a week. Treat her as you normally would, and you don't have to bring up the name change. If she mentions it, feel free to discuss it with her."

I sat at the nurse's station waiting for my mother to finish talking to my doctor. I knew she would fill my mother's head with bullshit, that cold-blooded bitch. She didn't give a damn about what I was going through. She approved of my therapist keeping me drugged up. She was one of those book smart bitches who didn't have a clue about real life shit.

During our first session, Dr. Montgomery asked me the meaning of the word crazy. I told her it was the new normal. Everyone deals with some form of mental challenge. If something takes you out of your normal and affects you emotionally, it can make you crazy. She told me having a weak mind makes you crazy. She said if life gives you lemons, you make lemonade. I told her I didn't know how to make lemonade from the death of my friend. I didn't know how to make lemonade from the attempted murder of my brother. The lemonade I'd make would be bitter. She told me I was missing the point of the exercise and I needed to think about it further. She expected me to have a better answer at our next visit. I knew she was a quack when she used lemonade to reference life situations.

I became impatient waiting for my mother after being locked up in this dog cage for almost a month. I was ready to get the hell out of there. I wanted to visit Derrick at the hospital. I decided to go and say my goodbyes to Gabby. Actually, her name was Gabriela. She was my new best friend. I called her Gabby because she talked so damn much. She was Hispanic. She stood 5'9" and weighed about 230 pounds. She was a big girl, but a beautiful girl. She told me she used to weigh 110 pounds, but she put on the extra weight in hopes that her mother's boyfriend, Juan, would stop molesting her.

Juan started touching her at the young age of ten. Gabby's mother made the mistake of leaving her at home with him while she went to work. Juan would go into Gabby's room when she was sleeping. He'd put his hands under the covers and rub on her arms and legs. He told Gabby it was a massage. The more comfortable he became with touching her, the more aggressive he got. He stopped touching her arms and legs and began touching her private parts. Juan told her that his behavior was normal. The fool even told her that in his country, the mother's boyfriend was considered the daughter's boyfriend, too.

After being molested for five years, Gabby started having panic attacks. It had become harder for her to cope with the abuse. By the time Gabby was fifteen, she had gained all the weight.

Her mother was too wrapped up with her boyfriend to pay attention to her daughter's excessive weight gain and her continuous panic attacks. Gabby told me her story the first day I was allowed in general population.

Gabby started sleeping in her clothes to discourage Juan from touching her. It worked at first, but then that nasty pedophile bastard walked in on her taking a shower. He grabbed her by her hair, threw her down on the floor, and pushed himself inside her. He mutilated her young womb.

Gabby's mother came home to find her lying on her bed with a blood-soaked towel between her legs. She had the nerve to be mad at Gabby for staining the towel. Instead of asking Gabby what happened, she assumed that Gabby had started her period. Gabby believed her mother knew that Juan had raped her. She could see that something was physically wrong with her. Anyone could have....

Gabby was now seventeen years old, and Juan had been molesting her for seven years. After he raped her, he continued to violate her.

Finally, she couldn't take it anymore. She found the courage to confide in her mother about the constant molestation. She thought if she told her mother what Juan had done, he would immediately be kicked out of the house.

Instead of her mother getting angry with Juan, she became angry with Gabby. She called her a liar and slapped her in the face. She accused her of being a whore. She called Gabby a fat cow, and picked up an empty beer bottle and hit her in the head with it.

"There's no way Juan would choose your fat ass over me."

Gabby snapped, grabbed her mother, and dragged her into the bathroom while punching her in the face. She put her head over the toilet bowl and shouted, "You've constantly treated me like I'm a piece of shit. I'm your daughter, and you should believe me. I have watched Juan abuse you. I've gotten out of bed before school to collect plastic bottles to help you make ends meet while Juan sleeps. He's abusing me. I'm no longer a little girl—he stole that from me many years ago.

Now I'm going to drown you in this toilet. I want you to know what it feels like to be me!"

Gabby pushed her mother's head into the toilet water and held her down with all her strength. Juan came into the bathroom, grabbed Gabby by the hair, and threw her to the floor. As Juan was walking out with Gabby's mother, she jumped on his back and tried to scratch his eyes out. Juan backed Gabby into the wall and hit her in the face, knocking her unconscious.

That night, Gabby woke up to Juan having sex with her. After he finished, she went into the bathroom, took a razor, and slit her wrist. She was admitted to the psych ward with a seventy-two-hour hold. Her mother signed the papers to have her committed.

Gabby will be released at the end of the month. Her mother visits on occasions, but only to persuade her not to bring charges against Juan. Her mother was a thirsty backyard dog that should've been put out of her misery.

"Eh la muchacha ¿cómo estás?" (Hey girl, how you doing?) I asked Gabby.

"Soy buena Tempestuoso Llu Via. El español es cada Vez major." (I'm good, Stormi Rain. Your Spanish is getting better.)

"Have you been released yet?"

"Yes, I have, but I'm waiting for my mother to finish talking to the doctor. You have my phone number and address. As soon as they release you, call me. We'll get together."

"Stormi Rain, I'll be living with my grand-mother. They won't release me to my mother."

"Is your mother's boyfriend still living with her?"

"Yes, she refuses to put him out."

"Your mother is a puta."

"I know."

"I have to go, but I'll see you at the end of the month when they release you."

"Goodbye, Stormi Rain."

"Adios."

I hugged Gabby. She reminded me of Shannon. She was nice, sweet, and innocent. It's hard to believe she lived through seven years of molestation before trying to kill herself. It was like being with Shannon all over again. They both lived with an unthinkable violation.

People can be cruel to one another. What gives a person the right to violate another person's body?

As I was walking toward the reception area, I could see my mother standing there waiting on me. I was happy to see her. I ran and gave her a big hug.

"Stormi, are you ready to go home, baby girl?"

"Yes, ma'am, but I want to see Derrick first. How's he doing?"

"He's holding his own, but I know God is going to restore him. I'll tell you all about it once we get into the car."

The last time I saw Derrick, he was lying in the street with blood oozing from his body and Asia was trying to get him to breathe.

I walked away because I thought he was dead.

As we walked to the car, my mother was praising and thanking God for my release and Derrick's recovery. She's a big believer that God will fix everything.

Where was her God when Derrick was shot down in the street? Where was her God when Shannon blew her head off and splattered her brain all over my face? Where was He when baby Joy was given iodine and her precious little heart blew up? Where was He when Juan ruptured Gabby's hymen, destroying her virgin womb?

I don't want to hear about her God.

THEY CALL ME STORMI RAIN

4

GIVE MY BROTHER BACK TO ME

We arrived at the hospital to visit Derrick. As I walked into his room, I saw he was being kept alive by several machines. I fell to my knees. I started to pray and beg God to heal him.

"God, please give my brother back to me. I'm trusting in your word. You are full of mercy and grace. Please forgive us for our sins and work a miracle to heal my brother in the name of Jesus."

My mother would always tell me it's in your praise. Before I knew it, I was in full worship. Thank you, Lord, for the healing. My natural instinct was to pray, but there was a battle going on in my head.

Stormi Rain: Your so-called prayers are falling on deaf ears. Get up off your knees and stop this prayer mess. Did you forget you have changed partners? You now dance with the darkness.

I stood there shaking, fighting the urge to pray. My heart dropped into my stomach. I was in a full-blown panic attack, and I felt the need to throw up. I didn't know what to do. I ran out of the room with tears streaming down my face.

My body was numb. I felt dead inside and I wanted to give up. My palms were sweaty and my heart was racing. All of a sudden, I felt the cold wind blow.

"God, is that you? What do you want with me? I refuse to pray to you. I refuse to trust you. I refuse to follow you."

My heart had been broken. The thought of living this life without Derrick was too much pain for me to tolerate. I needed help. I started running through the hospital grabbing any doctor I saw, begging them to help my brother.

My mother ran to find me. Once she did, she held me in her arms and started to pray.

"Baby girl, you have to learn to trust God. Do not allow your emotions to overtake you. This will get you nowhere. Stop and listen to His voice. He will lead, guide, and direct you. His ways are not our ways. His thoughts are not our thoughts. He is not going to respond to your emotions. Faith and trust are what moves God."

There was something about my mother's voice that was calming. I felt the cold wind blow again and instantly stopped crying. I walked back in the room to see Derrick. I leaned over, kissed him, and rubbed his head. After sitting for several hours, hoping my brother would wake, my mother told me it was time to go.

On our way home, we talked about my hospital stay. She wanted to know how I was feeling. I knew deep down inside she realized her little girl had a mental problem, but she wouldn't give up on me. My mother knew me better than anyone. She knew when I was feeling good and when I was feeling bad. The incident at the hospital, I believed, threw her for a loop. I had just been released and I was already running through the halls of a hospital. She was trying to see where I was mentally before we got home.

I wasn't taking the medication the doctor had prescribed for me, I only pretended to. In my sessions with Dr. Montgomery, she taught me how to recognize my triggers. She went over the things that had taken place before I had been committed.

She told me that after Derrick was shot, I wasn't lucid, I was irrational. I hadn't slept for three days, and no matter what my mother told me, I believed Derrick was dead. My mind had temporarily shut down. I didn't talk or eat for days at a time. My mother constantly prayed and anointed my head with oil.

One day as I sat staring out the window, a car backfired. The sound reminded me of the gunshot I heard when Derrick was shot. This threw me into an agitated state.

I left the house and ended up walking to the church looking for Pastor Lewis. He was in his study. I kicked opened the door.

"Pastor Lewis, you believe in miracles, right? That Bible you're holding gives you all the answers. I need you to bring my brother back to life. I know you can do it. I want you to find the scripture in the Bible where Lazarus was brought back

to life and I want you to do the same for my brother."

Pastor Lewis prayed for me, and then he anointed my head with oil. I thought he was trying to hurt me. I grabbed him by his neck and started choking him.

They tell me I could have been charged with attempted murder. Instead, I was admitted to the psychiatric hospital. I had a nervous breakdown.

"I think I better take my meds!"

THEY CALL ME STORMI RAIN

5

STORMI COMES HOME

As soon as I walked through the door, I saw my oldest brother, Matthew. He came home from college when he heard about Derrick. Matthew received a basketball scholarship and was hoping to play professionally when he graduated.

Our parents wanted him to go to medical school. Matthew was very smart. He always talked about becoming a doctor when he was younger. No one knew he could even play basket-ball. His senior year of high school he went out for the basketball team and became an overnight sensation. He was 6'5," weighed about 230 pounds, and was extremely handsome. He had the same problem my father had—the women loved him and would do anything to be with him. The hoes just wouldn't leave him alone.

"Hey, little sis, how are you feeling?"

"I'm feeling much better, now that they let my crazy ass out."

"You picked the wrong time to joke."

"Who's joking? I'm telling you the truth."

"Did Mom take you to see Derrick?"

"Yeah, she did."

"Okay, well, I'm on my way to visit with him. I will talk to you when I get back. Oh yeah, Justin's in the den waiting to see you, so cut the bullshit. Asia and Valencia are very emotional, and

Miles has been trying to keep himself busy. Keep everything together until I get back."

"Okay, will do."

I wasn't expecting to see Justin this soon. They didn't allow me to have visitors at the crazy house—only my parents were allowed to see me. My appearance was tore up from the floor up.

I walked into my bedroom before going to the den to see Justin, and in walked Valencia right behind me. She was all smiles.

"Stormi, you're home!"

She walked up and hugged me tight.

"Yes, Val, I am. What's been going on?"

"Why did you call me Val?"

"It's time for you to have a nickname, and I think Val fits you."

My sister, Valencia, was a sweet and loving little girl, although she wasn't so little anymore. Time sure had flown. I remembered taking her and Asia to the park to swing. Felt like yesterday.

Valencia was now in junior high school. Her long, black, silky hair and beautiful mocha complexion made her look as though she was of Indian decent. People would always question if she was my sister and I would get so fucking mad. My father was light, bright, and damn near white, and my mother was mocha brown just like Val. So, of course, they got a beautiful bouquet of children. Val's eyes sparkled like the stars in the sky, and her smile could melt your heart (as it does mine).

"Okay, Stormi, if you think I need a nickname, that's okay with me. I just might like being called Val. It could stand for valiant."

"Girl, it can stand for whatever you want it to. Matthew tells me Justin is here."

"He's sitting in the den waiting for you."

"I can't let him see me looking like this."

"No need to play games, Stormi. It is what it is. If he cares about you, it won't matter what you look like."

"Well, I'll soon find out."

I walked down the hallway to the den and saw Justin sitting on the couch reading a book. That's just like him to be reading or studying. He's so damn smart.

"Hey, Justin."

"Stormi, you've finally arrived. I've been waiting for two hours to see you."

"I'm sorry it took a long time for me to get home, but I had to stop by the hospital to see Derrick."

"No problem."

Justin grabbed me and kissed me on the cheek, holding me tight for a long time. I felt myself starting to get emotional. I pushed back and he released me.

I couldn't afford to let my emotions get the best of me. When you become emotional, you get weak. I had to remain strong. I had work to do. The person that shot my brother was going to pay. I had thought about nothing but revenge while I was mentally and physically incarcerated.

"Justin, give me a minute. I need to change clothes and freshen up."

"Sure."

I walked into my bedroom and was greeted by Asia.

"Hello, Stormi."

"Hey, Asia. What's going on with you?"

"I'm mad."

"About what?"

"I haven't been able to see Derrick since he's been in the hospital. I have to be eighteen. I don't think it's fair. After all Derrick and I have been through, I should be allowed to see him. I've done a lot of thinking since Derrick got hurt, and I decided I want to be a nurse."

"Asia, you're right. You should become a nurse. You pushed me out of the way and blew breath into Derrick's lungs without hesitation. I thought he died, but you helped him live."

"God allowed him to live."

"Did God allow him to get shot?"

"Girl, get out of my face talking stupid!"

"You're the one talking stupid. God did this and God did that. The bottom line is, Derrick's in the hospital and nothing is going to change that. Justin is waiting on me. I have to get my ass in the bathroom and put on some decent clothes. I'll take you and Val to see Derrick later."

"Who's Val?"

"That's the nickname I gave Valencia."

"Oh, okay. Every time you come back it's something new with you. For once, can you just come home and be normal?"

"I'm normal. You may not think so, little sister, but trust me, I am. I don't fit what society deems normal, but that's okay. I'm happy with who I am. I will continue to do what works for me."

"Okay, well does it work for you that your boyfriend took your cousin, Brittany, to the prom?"

"What are you talking about?"

"No one told you that Brittany and Justin went to the prom together?"

"Nope."

"You look a little puzzled. Are you mad, Stormi?"

"No, I'm not mad. I don't get mad. I get even."

"What does that mean?"

"It means whatever you want it to mean."

"Well, Stormi, you appear a little unnerved. Just know that Brittany did it for you. She didn't want Justin to go with anyone else, so she represented for you."

Wow, I wonder whose bright idea that was. I don't care that she's my cousin. Did anyone even think to ask me? Of course not, that would be too much like the right thing to do. People make deci-sions without considering how it's going to affect the other person. I trust no bitch.

"I'm not mad, Asia. I just don't like surprises. Someone should have told me. Damn, did she wear my dress, too?"

"Actually, she did."

Ain't that a bitch! Had everyone lost their minds? What would make them think it was okay for her to wear my dress? I bet everyone thought it would be another year before I'd be released. I guess I shouldn't be mad—maybe it worked in my favor. He could have taken someone else.

I came out the bathroom feeling refreshed. It was time for me to talk with Justin. I was con-cerned about Justin and Brittany going to the prom together, but how Justin felt about me being com-mitted outweighed the prom ordeal.

"Justin, how was the prom? I hear Brittany was your date. How did that happen?

"Um, I'm not really sure. I was told that Brittany would be my date because you weren't going to be released in time. I just went with the flow. Your family was acting like you being committed was no big deal. I knew you were having a hard time with Derrick being shot, but I didn't know that it affected you so deeply. Asia called and told me you were hospitalized. She also told me about Shannon and her baby. You and I had spoken briefly about it. Asia helped me understand what you were going through. Brittany and I have been friends for such a long time, she's like my sister. I felt it was a good move."

"You're right, it was a good move. Did you take her to the after prom?"

"No, I took her home and went to the after prom alone. I met up with some of my friends that had gone stag. By the way, I ran into your friend, Trent."

"What? Why was he at the after prom?"

"He knows some of the guys I run track with. Actually, he supplies them with steroids to help them run faster."

"What? Justin, you stay away from him. He's no good."

"Stormi, I'm not worried about that dude. I can handle myself. I'll be all right. He seems cool. I did ask him about the debt he said you owed, and he told me not to worry about it—that it wasn't a big deal."

"Is that really all he told you?"

"Yeah, is there more to the story?"

"Yes, Justin, there's a lot more to the story, but now's not the time to discuss it. Just stay away from him. He may be the one that shot Derrick."

"Stormi, that dude didn't have anything to do with Derrick being shot. At least I don't think so."

"How would you know?"

"Because when I was being interviewed by the police, I overheard them talking about that lady named Babette—the one that was standing outside the house when Derrick was shot. She's their primary suspect."

"What? I didn't know that."

"You did just get home, Stromi."

I couldn't believe that crazy woman might be the one that shot my brother. All this time I was thinking it was Trent. This was my fault. I should've handled her when I had the chance. Now Derrick was fighting for his life because I didn't take care of her ass when I should've.

"Has she been arrested?"

"I don't know. I overheard them saying she was a suspect. I don't know if they have sufficient evidence to arrest her. I haven't heard anything. But on another note, I wanted to talk to you about school."

"What about school, Justin?"

"I'm going to be leaving after graduation to check out Florida State University. I know that with everything going on with Derrick, you may not be able to go with me."

"You're right. I won't be able to go. As a matter of fact, I probably won't be able to attend the first year. I may need to stay home and help my mother take care of Derrick. I'm sure she's going to need help with him."

"Stormi, I understand. You do what you need to do. We will work through this together. Things will work out for the best."

Justin looked into my eyes and kissed me. He was a nice guy. There were times I thought he was too good to be true. He was smart, funny, handsome, and respectful. He never tried to touch my jewel box, and I often wondered why.

If he wasn't getting my jewel box, whose jewel box was he getting? I wasn't going to let him leave for school and not feel my warm insides.

THEY CALL ME STORMI RAIN

THINGS WOULD NEVER BE THE SAME

After all my family had been through, I still had to graduate. I didn't want to participate in my graduation ceremony; after all, it was just a piece of paper. But me walking across that stage meant the world to Mother. When I was committed the first time, people didn't really talk about it. They just stared at me most of the time. It really didn't matter because most of them were my clientele and all they cared about was getting high. But when you've been committed twice—you become the topic of discussion. Not only do they stare, they have the nerve to ask you dumb ass questions. "Do you feel like you want to kill yourself?" or "What does it feel like to be crazy?" People can be cruel. No one thinks before they speak. They feel it's okay to say whatever pops into their head. I never told my mother how I felt about participating in the ceremony. She had no idea what I dealt with when I was at school. Because it meant so much to my mother, and she meant so much to me, I agreed to walk at graduation. My mother was so excited; she planned a graduation party at the house. My cousins and a few friends attended. After a couple hours of entertaining, I wanted to take a walk and get some air. I felt smothered by all the questions and the staring. I knew they were thinking that I had been released too early. When I had my first breakdown, it took me a year to recover. I walked to the store around the corner from the house.

As I approached, I saw King's crazy ass hanging out on the corner. I had to walk by him to enter. As I approached, that motherfucka had the balls to speak to me. I ignored him, which made him angry. He kept talking and I kept walking. Finally, he said something that struck a nerve.

He said I should have been committed to the looney bin for life. He continued to talk about how I lied about him raping Shannon, and how I tried to make people believe that Shannon's baby was his.

Stormi Rain: Stay calm; the day will come when he will pay for his actions, but not now.

"King, you're pushing your luck. If Shannon's name comes out of your mouth again, we're going to have a big problem."

"Stormi, you're crazy and everyone knows it. I ain't scared of you. I will fuck you just like I fucked your dead ass friend."

My blood was boiling. I was beyond mad; I was at the point of no return. I felt this was my moment to settle the score. I wanted to bite King in his face and not let go. I had already pictured in my mind so many times what I would do to him, and biting him in the face wasn't enough. I had to be smart and do something that would last a lifetime. He would pay for all the hurt and harm he has caused.

I decided not to let him take me out of character. If I moved too soon, things wouldn't go as planned.

Control yourself, do not forget where you come from. You are covered with the blood of Jesus. The word of God says in Romans 12:19, "Beloved, do not avenge yourselves, but rather give place to the wrath; for it is written, 'Vengeance is Mine, I will repay,' says the Lord."

"King, my apologies. I don't know what I was thinking. I had no right to tell people you raped

Shannon, and we all know Joy wasn't your daughter."

"Yeah, well, you did. And some of the people from the neighborhood stopped dealing with me because of your lies. You fucked my life up, you and your dead friend."

"Trust me, King, my plan is to make it all better. The day will come when I will fix all the wrongdoings. Just give me time. I assure you, my plan is to make your life better."

"Bitch, get out of my face."

I walked into the store. It took everything in me not to respond to King's ugly ass. I wanted to, but I knew I needed to be careful. I couldn't let him push my buttons.

I put my soda on the counter. That's when I heard, someone say, "It's on me."

I turned and saw Reese standing there. "Hey, let me take care of that for you."

I'm thinking to myself, what the hell is going on? Why are two of my worst enemies confronting me? I stood there looking Reese up and down. She couldn't possibly be talking to me.

"Stormi, it's been a long time. How are you doing?"

"I'm doing just fine, Reese."

I looked at the cashier and told her I'd be paying for my own soda.

Reese followed me out of the store. She continued to talk and I continued to ignore her.

Did this bitch forget we're not friends? I'm confused as to why she thinks we could have a conversation.

"Stormi, wait a minute. I want to talk to you."

"About what?"

"I just wanted to tell you I'm sorry about what happen to your brother. Is there anything I could do to help?"

"What could you do to help my brother? You're not a doctor. You're not a specialist. What do you think you have to offer?"

"Stormi, all I have to give is my support. I've wanted to apologize to you for all my wrongdoings. I had been seeing James for months before he started seeing you. I knew he was just using you. I tried to tell you but you wouldn't listen. You continued to see him and I became jealous. When I found out King raped Shannon, I had to honor the no snitch code of the neighborhood. I wanted to prove my loyalty to James. When you and I had that fight, I knew I'd have James for myself. But even though you were out the picture, he still played around on me. I forgot all about being a friend to you and Shannon, and I'll regret that for the rest of my life. I'm sorry and ashamed of myself. Will you please forgive me? I know I can't change what happened, but if you give me a second chance I'd like to start our friendship over."

I looked at Reese with so much hate in my heart.

Stormi Rain: People should think before they do things. For every one of you ignorant bastards that fucked with me, there's a crazy spell with your name on it.

"Reese, I'm not sure if I'm ready to work on our friendship. We've gone through a lot and you've done some things that I feel are unforgivable."

"I have many sleepless nights. I miss Shannon, too. She was just as much my friend as yours. I feel so sad about her death and her baby. I'm not heartless! I'm turning my life around. I'm going to church and working on becoming a much better person. The word of God says in 1 John 1:9, 'If we confess our sins, he is faithful and just and will forgive us our sins and purify us from all unrighteousness.'"

"Well, Reese, I'm not God, so don't look to me for what you're supposed to get from him. You say you feel bad, but it's too late for that. Shannon's dead and so is Joy. Your feelings are not a factor for me. I'm going to keep moving. See you in traffic."

The nerve of some people. Just because you want to make peace with God doesn't give you the right to include me in your mission. I felt myself becoming overwhelmed with memories of the past and the people who were still around to remind me. I tried to remain calm, but some days were harder than others. I went to therapy once a week. It was supposed to help keep my mind intact. My mother was constantly praying and quoting scriptures. Little did she know she was a day late and a dollar short trying to save me.

I couldn't be saved. I had already sold my soul to the devil. I was just waiting for the opportunity to fuck some shit up.

Things would never be the same.

THEY CALL ME STORMI RAIN

7

DERRICK WAKES UP

After being in a coma for over a month, Derrick woke up and was moved to a rehabilitation center. Derrick being awake gave my mother life. It was the answer to her prayers. The doctors had told her it would only be a matter of time before he'd die. They kept trying to get her to pull the plug, but she wouldn't. She'd tell them, "It's not over until God says it's over. I trust God."

Yeah, I remember saying those same words once upon a time. "I trust God." But not anymore. I don't trust anyone but myself.

The doctors didn't know Derrick had a brain injury until he woke up. He hit his head when he hit the ground after being shot. He had problems communicating and he could barely feed himself. He tried walking, but he had problems with his right leg. He had a speech therapist and a physical therapist. The speech therapist was making progress with him, but his physical therapist was a joke.

It was hard seeing him struggle to walk. I promised I'd get him the best therapist money could buy. I had to get back out into the streets and start doing what I did best. I had to put together another money team. Gabby was going to be released in two weeks, and she'd be a great addition. With Brittany and her working together, it would double sales.

When Derrick came out of his coma, my mother decided to tell us that Babette was arrested for the shooting. She was facing life in prison. She also informed us that Babette had a son that was our little brother. My father had a paternity test taken, and the test came back positive. He was the father. Even though my father was a cheater, he never neglected his fatherly duties. He always took care of our home. Because that little boy had my father's blood running through his veins, he wanted my mother to consider taking in his bastard child.

I asked my mother if she was actually thinking about it. She told me that she had prayed about it and was waiting to hear from the Lord. I couldn't believe my mother was considering taking in this kid. I asked her not to play superwoman. My father stuck his pole of life into someone else, and my mother was going to have to pay the price of his infidelity.

My mother had a heart like no other; she could always find the good in a bad situation.

Well, I hoped her God wasn't going to have her take in the bastard child. Her son was lying in a hospital bed recovering from a gunshot wound from the bastard's mother. I think it would be in the best interest of the child if he remained in foster care. They better keep him away from here before he comes up missing.

THEY CALL ME STORMI RAIN

8

THE SNOW BUNNY

Derrick needed a therapist, so I had to go back to hustling. But first, I had to get approval from Trent. The last time I saw Trent, I was begging him to have Derrick's back. I had stopped hustling and wanted Derrick to do the same, but he refused. With me preparing to go away to school, I had to ensure Derrick's safety. Trent was already mad at me for not taking him up on his offer. He wanted to follow me to school so he could take care of me. He told me he loved me. When I told him I didn't feel the same and that I was with Justin, he hung up the phone and we didn't speak again. The next time I saw Trent, I was standing in the middle of his bedroom, butt naked with honey dripping down my body. I left that night trusting Trent would look out for Derrick.

It was a relief that Trent had nothing to do with the shooting. There were only two people outside at the time Derrick was shot—Babette and Trent. I was sure that Trent was the one that had shot Derrick. I would have bet money on it. This made my life much easier; I would hate to have to hurt someone that I considered a friend. I borrowed my mother's car and headed to Trent's house. Once I arrived, I saw him standing outside talking to a snow bunny.

What's this white girl doing in our neighborhood?

I got out of the car and walked up the driveway where they were standing.

"Hey, Trent."

"Stormi, what's up, girl? I heard you had been released. I was wondering when I was going to see you. How's your brother?"

"He's not doing that great. I came by so we can talk business. You got a couple minutes you can spare?"

"Yeah, sure. I'll make time for you. Just let me see my girl off. Oh, by the way, this is Jessica. Jessica, this is Stormi."

Did he just call her his girl? What's going on?

"Hello, Stormi. It's nice to make your acquaintance."

"Hello." *Is this bitch serious?*

"I'll walk Jessica to her car and then we can talk."

"Okay."

They stood talking for another five minutes by her car. Trent kissed her and then she drove away.

Trent ran up, grabbed me, and started playing around.

"What can I do for you, Stormi?"

"Trent, I need some work. I need to make some serious money. Derrick needs a better therapist than the one he has, and it takes money to get the best. I have some money saved, but not enough."

"What's wrong with the therapist he has?"

"He has a good speech therapist, but his physical therapist is a joke. Derrick can barely walk. He still drags his right leg. He's not getting any better. I've found one of the top therapists in the city, and she said she could get him back to normal. It's going to cost a lot because she's a private provider. The insurance my parents have won't cover her fees."

"Well, Jessica's my top seller now. I'm not sure there's room for you."

"Ain't this a bitch! You have to be kidding me. There's always room for Stormi! She can't outsell me. My money team is ready to go. We can outsell your snow bunny any day."

"I don't think so. I'm pushing a new product and it's just now getting to our neighborhood. The white neighborhoods already have it."

"What are you talking about?"

"I'm talking about that white powder—cocaine! Your customer base is weed and black mollies. You're not ready for this. How much money do you need?"

"Twenty thousand."

"Well, I can loan it to you if you want."

"How long do I have before I have to pay you back?

"That's up to you."

"Trent, I know you're not going to let me take my time and pay you back. There's more to this, I'm sure."

Trent opened the front door to his house and walked in. I followed behind him. I took a seat in the living room. He went to his bedroom. Of course, he came back with some hash. I hadn't smoked since I'd been with Justin. I cut all that out once I decided to turn my life around. I wasn't sure if I wanted to smoke, but I didn't think I had a choice. I knew Trent was expecting me to smoke with him.

Stormi Rain: "Do what you have to do to get what you want. You knew what to expect when you decided to come see Trent. Let's not play games; you're either all in or you're out. You can't have it both ways. You made your choice when you decided to walk on the dark side. Pull yourself together and do what's necessary to get what you want, that's how the game is played. You have to give to get. Give him something he will never forget. Lay his ass out.

Trent fired up the hash, and I took a long hard drag. My body had been craving it. I was high and it felt good. I was grooving to the music that was playing on the stereo. I felt very sexy. My jewel box began to throb. I put my foot in between Trent's legs and began to rub between his thighs. I could feel his pole of life growing in size. Trent ignored my sexual gestures. He didn't respond and I was instantly irritated. I refused to be defeated. I got up, pulled my top off, and danced around for him in my bra. He still didn't respond.

Trent sat on the couch and didn't say a word. *I'll show him!* I pulled my pants down and got butt ass naked, then I bent over and spread my butt cheeks in his face. I took my finger and rubbed my jewel box until I felt the sweet drippings of my hot juices. Trent stared at me, but didn't say a word. He talked to me with his eyes. He knew he wanted to lay that pipe, but he was playing hard to get. I stopped dancing around, picked up my clothes, and headed to the bathroom. I splashed my face with cold water and pulled myself together. It was obvious he was playing games. I was bothered by the rejection, but I soon realized it was all about control with Trent.

After getting my emotions together in the bathroom, I walked out and sat on the couch. I told him I had to go home, but that I'd be back tomorrow to let him know if I was going to take the loan. I leaned over and kissed him on the cheek before walking out the door. I had to think long and hard about accepting the money from Trent. I knew there would be a price to pay. While driving home, I thought about how I allowed myself, once again, to fall right back into the arms of Trent.

I was comfortable with him. We had a great connection, but I was actually in love with Justin.

THEY CALL ME STORMI RAIN

9

I Miss You Shannon

I got home and took a nice hot bath. I had to prepare for my date with Justin. I was glad that I didn't have sex with Trent, otherwise I would've been feeling like a hoe. My mind drifted off to thoughts of Shannon. I imagined Shannon and me sitting in her bedroom listening to music. I would've been able to tell her about the mistake I almost made with Trent. We'd be laughing about it. I missed my best friend. I couldn't hold back my tears; before I knew it, I was boohooing like a baby.

I slipped down under the water to muffle my cries. I wanted to talk to Shannon. I figured I would go and visit her grave before my date with Justin. I finished my bath and got dressed.

I put a blanket in the car, pulled some flowers from our garden in the front yard, and drove to the cemetery. Once I arrived, I sat in the car staring at all the headstones. It was creepy being surrounded by dead people. I walked to Shannon's gravesite. I laid my blanket out and sat down. I placed the flowers on her headstone.

"Hey, best friend. I hope all is well with you and Joy. I know you're just walking around Heaven having a good time. I just wanted to come and talk to you. I see your mother from time to time, but she doesn't say much. Maybe you should pay her a visit to let her know you're all right. It will help her move on. If I didn't have you visiting

me from time to time, I would ball up and die. Your spirit keeps me alive. I always feel better when I visit with you."

I felt warm and cozy. I knew it was Shannon letting me know she was there. I got comfortable, laid down on the blanket, and closed my eyes. I started to daydream about all the fun Shannon and I used to have when we were kids. Oh, how I wished I could go back in time. Visiting Shannon made me feel normal. It gave me a sense of security. I could be free with my feelings. I didn't have to worry about being judged. I felt such peace being at Shannon's gravesite, and I knew she and Joy were present.

I felt a nudge on my shoulder. I jumped up. It was the cemetery attendant waking me.

"Ma'am, are you okay?"

"Yes, I'm fine. I just drifted off."

"The visiting hours are over. I'm afraid I'm going to have to ask you to leave."

"It's okay. It's time for me to go anyway."

I got into my car and headed to Justin's house. While driving, I thought about how nice it would be to be with Shannon on a permanent basis. My life had been so stressful. At times, I wanted to give up. The thought of running the car into a brick wall had crossed my mind. I just couldn't bring myself to do it. I was a coward. Maybe one day I'd have the courage.

I began to feel better once I pulled into Justin's driveway. I took a deep breath and got out of the car. I saw Justin standing on the porch waiting for me with a big smile. Suddenly, the anxiousness in my stomach disappeared.

"Hello, Stormi."

"What's up, Justin?"

"You're what's up. Let's get this date started."

Justin grabbed me, held me tight, and kissed me on my forehead. I loved when he did that. It made all the bad feelings go away. I was looking forward to our night out. I just wanted to be wrapped up in his arms, hugging and kissing him. I was curious about where we were going. Instead of trying to take control, I sat back and allowed Justin to handle our date.

He took me to the pier for dinner and the arcade afterwards. We walked around the pier and enjoyed the fresh air. He even bought me flowers from one of the vendors. We were having an awesome time, but it was getting late and it was time to go home. When we walked to the car, Justin opened my door. He was such a gentleman.

On our way back to Justin's house, he mentioned his parents were out for the evening. I knew what that meant—we were finally going to be together. When we arrived, he got out and opened my door. He grabbed my hand, escorting me to my car. He kissed me gently again on the forehead and told me he'd see me tomorrow.

What the hell? I needed to release some frustration. A good nut would do the trick. Trent wouldn't soothe me, and now Justin's sending me on my way, too. No one wants to make love or fuck me. Either one would do.

———◆———

After a good night's sleep, I came to my senses. I can always take care of myself. That's the one thing James taught me. I'm my own pleasure principle. I allowed my emotions to get the best of me yesterday. I had never seen Trent with anyone, so I got jealous when I saw him with his snow bunny. There were too many emotions attached to working with Trent. The more I thought about it, I knew it wasn't a good idea for me to borrow money from him. I'd rather work for it. I wasn't going to get caught up in a trick bag and sleep with him, and then still have to pay the loan back. My jewel box isn't free—you have to pay the cost to be the boss. I was so glad I came to my senses.

Stormi Rain: "You sound like a stupid ass little girl. Boss up and be the bad ass chick you are. You don't have time for games. Everything has to be on your terms. That's when you know you're winning. You have the power to control a man's mind. You fuck when you want to—and only when you want to. Trent showed that he's in control by not touching you, and you had the nerve to get upset. It's all about control. Don't let your cravings for someone else's body control your actions! You will get yourself into a world of hurt by responding to emotions. Always stay ahead of the game. Your pussy responds to touch, and no one can touch it better than you can. Take care of your own needs and desires. Let's keep moving forward with our plans. It's time to get even with all those who have wronged you and Shannon."

———— ◆ ————

I was lying in bed thinking about my next move when the phone rang.

"Stormi, baby, how you doing?"

"Hey, Trent. What's up?"

"Well, I wanted to know what you decided. I need to pull the money together if you're going to take the loan."

"I think I'm going to wait. That's a lot of money to borrow from you and I don't want to mess up our friendship."

"Look, Stormi. We've always had a great friendship. Money has never been an issue for us. You need the money and I have it. There's no pressure on paying me back."

"I know, but things have changed. I'm involved with Justin now and you're involved with Jessica, so we actually don't have the same relationship."

"Stormi, I still love you. I'll do anything for you. Jessica is just my employee."

"She's more than that, and you know it. But let me think about it. I have to go see Derrick this morning. Let me see how he's doing and I'll let you know."

"Okay."

I got off the phone with Trent and went to the bathroom. The phone rang again.

"Hello?"

"Hey, Stormi. What are you up to?"

"I'm going to visit with Derrick today. What's up with you?"

"Well, I know we have plans for tonight, but my boys want me to hang out with them before I leave for Florida tomorrow."

"What, so I'm not going to see you tonight?"

"If you don't mind, I'd like to hang out with my boys before I leave."

"Aww, is that right? You want to hang out with your boys? That's cool."

"I'll come by tomorrow morning before I leave."

"Okay, Justin, do you!"

I got off the phone mad as hell. Did he just pick his friends over me? What's going on? I'd never do that to him.

Stormi Rain: "Guard your heart. Not everyone loves the same. I think you care more for him than he cares for you. You have to find your balance. Only you can make yourself happy. Never leave your happiness to another person. This relationship with Justin is going to mess up our plans. Pull your shit together. No man is worth your tears."

Justin left for Florida without touching my jewel box.

What's wrong with him? I've tried to spread my legs for him on more than one occasion, but he didn't appear interested.

Our first time together was supposed to be prom night, but I didn't make it for reasons beyond my control. Justin had been acting a little strange. He was disappearing on occasion and looked like he was losing weight. I tried to talk to him about it, but he assured me everything was okay.

THEY CALL ME STORMI RAIN

10

THERAPY GONE WRONG

With Justin being gone, I had no one to talk to but Doctor Montgomery, my psychiatrist. I didn't want to talk to her, but I had no choice.

I couldn't talk to Gabby because she had a relapse. That bitch ass mother of hers came to visit and fucked with Gabby's headspace. She sat in the visiting room with Gabby, promising her everything was going to be different once she got home. She was still trying to convince Gabby not to press charges against Juan. When Gabby refused, she whispered in Gabby's ear, "*You fucking puta! I should've aborted your fat ass. I knew when I was carrying you that you'd be a pain in my culo. I never wanted a daughter. You're something that just happened, you loco perra!*"

As Gabby's mother spoke, she fell to the floor into the fetal position, convulsing as though she was having a seizure.

Gabby stopped all forms of communication. She sat and stared into space all day. The nurses had to help her bathe and eat.

I had to help Gabby return to somewhat normal behavior. You can only dwell in your genius for a short period. If you stay too long, there's no coming back. I had to bring her back to reality. We had work to do.

"Doctor Montgomery, when will my weekly visits stop?"

"Stormi, weekly therapy is a part of your treatment. It's necessary for your recovery."

"Doctor, you make it sound like I have an addiction. What do I need to recover from? I'm all good."

"No, you're not. You've had to deal with some major crises in your life, and it takes time to work through it."

"You mean to tell me talking to you is going to make me better?"

"Expressing your thoughts and emotions, instead of keeping them inside will help you release your anger. Eventually you'll understand that life is a rollercoaster ride, but you won't be on the rollercoaster forever."

"Doctor Montgomery, it sounds like you're saying life is fucked up. I could've told you that. Your job is easy. You just sit here all day listening to people's problems. You move your head every once and while and write some shit down on paper. I bet dealing with all these people has made you one crazy bitch!"

"Stormi, you need to watch your language."

"Why? It's no big deal. I'm sure you've heard worse. Are you really concerned with my language? I thought I was here because life became too hard for me. I use foul language because I want to. It makes me feel good. What do you want from me? There's no recovery for me. After seeing my best friend blow her brains out and my brother shot down in the street and left for dead, there's no coming back. Who recovers from things like that? I spend my days visiting my best friend and her daughter at the cemetery and watching my brother struggle to walk after my father's side bitch tried to take his life."

"Stormi, your time is up. I'll see you next week, same time."

"Bitch, did you just dismiss me? You just cut me off mid-sentence. You just sit here collecting a pay check, not helping anyone get better."

"Let me be clear. I have the power to release you or commit you. If you keep coming in here disrespecting me, I'll have your ass locked up. Don't let the fact that I'm a doctor make you think you can talk to me any way you want. You're not crazy, by far, but let me be blunt; I'll have you committed for life. That's the power I hold in my hands. I can diagnose you as clinically insane. The next time you walk through this door, you better think twice."

"11542 Morningside Lane. That's where you live with your two girls and your husband, right? You see, Doctor, I've learned early that most adults can't be trusted. Most people are self-absorbed takers, and they'll use you if you let them. When I arrived here, you treated me like all your other patients, even though my issues were different. You didn't care about what really happened to me; you just threw me in with everyone else. Your "one-for-all" approach isn't working. You're not seeing any of us as human beings. You only see mental conditions, which you treat with a textbook and a pill. During my recent stay, you never once came to my room to see how I was doing. I saw you once when I arrived. My therapist got pissed off because I called her a bitch, and she talked you into allowing her to strap me down for days. She'd stop by and peek in to see if I had given in yet. You're supposed to help me heal, but instead you're inflicting more pain. I knew you couldn't be trusted. People like you misuse their authority.

You have no idea what I'm capable of doing. You just made the wrong move. Checkmate, bitch!

A word of advice, don't leave your husband alone too much. He spends a lot of time at this coffee shop on Lankershirm. There's this cute little girl who makes his coffee just the way he likes it, and she has mo' ass and mo' tits than you do. I would check it out, if I were you. There will always be someone better looking than you. If you want to keep your man away from the forbidden fruit, I suggest you stop being a straight-laced bitch and learn a trick or two for your husband. Oh, yeah, I forgot—your time is up. I'll see you next week, Doctor Montgomery."

I really hated that I had to fuck up Doctor Montgomery's world, but she was asking for it. I have learned that some people don't know how to handle power. You always have to keep an ace in the hole for days like this.

THEY CALL ME STORMI RAIN

11

WHY IS DERRICK ON THE FLOOR?

When I left Doctor Montgomery's office, I headed to the rehabilitation center to see Derrick. When I arrived, I found Derrick lying on the floor of his room. I ran over to help him up, but he was too heavy for me to pick up by myself. I screamed for help and in waddles this fat ass nurse huffing and puffing.

I couldn't believe what I was seeing. She was breathing like she needed to be on a ventilator her damn self. She had to stop and catch her breath before we could get Derrick off the floor.

After we got him situated, the nurse apologized for her shortcomings. I wanted to accept her apology, but I couldn't pass up the chance to tell her how I felt. There was no way I'd let her get away with this.

"I'm sorry you had to help me with Derrick, but I have a touch of asthma. It kicks up sometimes when I exert myself."

"Hi, my name's Stormi. Derrick is my brother. What's your name?"

"Oh, silly me. My name is Nurse Victoria."

"That's good to know, because I thought your name was Nurse Dumbass. It's sad that you're in a health care profession and you can't take care of your patients. You said you have a touch of asthma; well, I think you have a touch of I can't close my mouth, so I put everything in it. I think you should come back to this profession after you've lost about 100 pounds. I have nothing against your size, but your inability to breathe normally after just walking into a room could be detrimental to your patients. I'll be requesting a new nurse, so please excuse yourself from my brother's room."

Nurse Dumbass walked out and I sat on the side of Derrick's bed.

"How did you end up on the floor?"

"I wanted to see if I could get out of the bed without help. I'm tired of being treated like I'm handicapped."

"I know, Derrick. It won't be much longer. I'm going to get you the best therapist money can buy."

"Thanks, but I don't want you doing anything crazy to take care of me."

"Don't you worry about me. I'll take care of everything and I won't have to do anything crazy."

I had to make sure Derrick had the best care possible. I hated the thought of going back out in the streets to hustle, but I had no choice.

"Derrick, do you remember what happened the night you were shot?"

"Not really. I keep seeing this woman in my dreams holding a little boy's hand. She walks up and shoots me. I have this dream every night."

"Dad's backyard dog, Babette, shot you. She has a child with Dad and she wanted him to be a part of our family. When Dad refused, her crazy ass shot you. I'm sorry, Derrick, for taking such a long time to tell you what happened, but the family felt it would be best to wait until you were better. We didn't want to risk upsetting you."

"Stormi, that's crazy. I really thought it had something to do with me being out working the streets. How did the police discover it was her?

"They were investigating the shooting and asked Mom for the names of anyone who may have had a problem with our family. Babette's name came up. She became a suspect because Dad had gotten an order of protection against her. She wasn't allowed to come within 100 feet of our house. She was also seen standing outside our house the day you were shot. The police questioned her whereabouts and her story didn't add up. They got a search warrant for her house and found the gun she shot you with."

"That's crazy."

"No, Derrick, what's crazy is Mom is considering taking in Babette's son to live with us."

"What? You can't be serious."

"I am. You know our mother, she feels sorry for him. He has no family and he's been put into foster care. She feels obligated because he's Dad's son."

"Stormi, this is too much for one day. I need to get some rest."

"Don't let this worry you. Just keep your head up. It's going to be all right. I'll get the money, and you'll get the therapy you need. I'll be back tomorrow to visit you."

"Bye, Stormi."

"Goodbye, Derrick."

Seeing Derrick on the floor made me more determined than ever to get him the best treatment money could buy. The only way I could do that was by taking Trent up on his offer. I was hesitant because I didn't have my money team ready to go, and that meant I'd have to do it by myself.

Stormi Rain: "Here you go again with that weak ass thinking. Get it together. You're good at what you do. If you continue to second-guess yourself, you're going to set yourself up for failure. Your main weakness is Justin. Stop being so emotional. I'm here to protect you, and we have a lot of work ahead of us. Payback is going to be a bitch. Let Justin go to school and you focus on

making your money. I don't think he likes pussy anyway. You better tune into what's going on around you. Learn to be a good listener. This is how you learn people's weaknesses."

I couldn't stand the thought of Derrick remaining in that rehabilitation center any longer, so I went to visit Trent. I pulled up to his house and, of course, Jessica was sitting on the porch. My skin was starting to itch just from the sight of her. I took a deep breath and tried to remain in control. I got out of the car and walked up to her.

"Is Trent home?"

"Yeah, he's here. He'll be right out. He had to take an important call."

I nodded my head and walked past her. I opened the door. She got up and watched me walk in, but she didn't say anything. The look on her face was priceless.

Stormi Rain: *This is your time to shine, put something on his mind!*

I walked through the living room and into the kitchen, but there was no sign of Trent. I heard music playing, so I followed the sounds to Trent's bedroom. I pushed opened the door and walked in. The music was coming from his bathroom. The bathroom door was cracked opened, so I stood quietly in the doorway watching him shower. Even with the steam on the glass door, I could see his beautiful body. I watched the water run down his perfectly chiseled chest. It brought back memories of the last time we made love.

He poured honey on my naked body as he grabbed me by my hair. He threw me on the bed and kissed me all over, paying special attention to the inner parts of my thighs. Then his pole of life stroked my jewel box.

As Trent rinsed his body, he opened his eyes to find me staring at him. He opened the shower door and stepped out, reaching for his dry towel. He looked at me and didn't say a word. He dried off and stood naked with his pole of life stretched out. I took a deep breath and walked over to him. I remained silent as I rubbed my hands down his chiseled chest. I kissed his chest softly before I sucked his nipples until they pointed to attention. I licked him up and down, moving slowly to the middle of his stomach. The closer I got to his pole of life, the more it stretched out. He ran his hands through my hair as he slightly pushed my head down closer to his pole of life. I could tell he was excited by the thought of my mouth moving closer.

As the intensity built, in walked Jessica. *Like I knew she would.* She was breathing extremely hard. I knew she was mad, but I remained calm. Trent stood fully stretched out. I looked at Jessica and signaled for her to come closer. Trent became more excited. I motioned for her to get on her knees. As she kneeled down, Trent's pole of life entered her mouth.

Stormi Rain: Checkmate, bitch. The only thing that goes in my mouth is food.

I moved out the way and let Jessica handle her business. I told Trent I'd call him later. I walked to the car knowing I won the game Trent was trying to play. I'm a better chess player than Jessica. The primary objective in chess is to obtain your opponent's king. When a king can't avoid capture, it's checkmate—the game is over.

Trent will never avoid capture when it comes to playing with me. I play to win. I gave Trent's snow bunny a run for her money. She got her ass handed to her. The sad part is, she didn't even know it. Dumbass!

THEY CALL ME STORMI RAIN

12

TIME TO MAKE A MOVE

With the loan from Trent, I was able to pay for Derrick's specialist. I had to confide in my older brother, Matthew, about what I was doing. He needed to help facilitate the specialist without our parents knowing who was paying for his therapy.

Matthew played basketball in college, so he knew several sport injury doctors. He told our parents he knew a doctor who was willing to help Derrick at no cost. Matthew explained that the doctor donated so many hours of therapy a year to people who couldn't afford his services. Without hesitation, our parents agreed to allow the doctor to help Derrick. They felt it was a blessing from the Lord.

Derrick's therapy was underway and he was making progress. As for Matthew, he contacted me once he returned to school to let me know he wanted to be paid for his services. I couldn't believe what I was hearing. My own brother was blackmailing me. He told me he was well aware of what I was doing and that it was illegal. He felt he should reap some reward because dealing with me made him an accomplice to my illegal gains.

I couldn't believe my brother was trying to pimp me. I'm going to let him think he got over on his little sister.

All that mattered to me was that Derrick was on the road to recovery and my beautiful mother was happy. She spent every waking moment making sure Derrick was okay.

It had been a long, hard road, but after months of therapy, Derrick was finally home. He was now able to walk without assistance.

Finally, I had time to think about what I wanted to do. It was time for me to make a move. I wasn't sure what direction I was headed in. I just knew I needed to do something for myself. I still wanted to attend Florida State University with Justin, but with me owing Trent money, going to school didn't appear to be in my near future. When Justin went to visit the University, he decided to stay and attend their summer program. His counselor helped him get into the program and they provided him with off-campus housing.

He surprised me with a plane ticket so I could visit him. When the ticket arrived, I looked at it several times before I put it in my dresser drawer. I struggled with the thought of going to Florida. I knew if I went to visit, I wouldn't want to come back. I needed to see Justin. Emotionally, I felt disconnected from him. I needed to see if I still felt the same way about our relationship.

Justin and I had lived very different lives, and for a brief moment, I thought I could change my path. Justin opened my eyes to a world of endless possibilities. I believed I could graduate from college and be successful.

Yeah, well, so much for that. Babette destroyed those dreams for me. That crazy backyard dog stole my future, and she was going to pay for it. The thought of having to go back to hustling made me sick to my stomach, but I had no choice. I had to cover my debt with Trent. I needed to put my money team back together.

My cousin, Brittany, had a love interest, so she wasn't ready to go back to hustling. She wanted to live a normal life that didn't consist of selling drugs. I understood because I felt the same way just a few months ago. The only other person I could count on was Gabby, but I had to wait for her to be released.

In the meantime, all I had was myself to count on.

Stormi Rain: Look, take a few days…. This chaos will be here when you get back. We have work to do, but your mind needs to be right. You don't want to have another psychotic break. Go visit Justin and relax so when you come back, you're ready to work. Right now, Trent is the least of your worries. He's not going to pressure you about the money. We'll work on the hit list when you get back.

I knew I was feeling overwhelmed. The thought of visiting a different state got me excited, so I decided to go. I should've been working on getting Trent his money. My intentions were to pay him back as soon as possible. I didn't want this arrangement to drag out for too long. I didn't like that I owed him, but I owed it to myself to stay sane. I decided to visit Justin. I would deal with Trent when I got back.

It took weeks of trying to convince my parents to allow me to go to Florida. One day, while I was sitting in the backyard soaking up some sun, my father approached me. We had a heart-to-heart; he apologized for all the hurt he caused. He explained that he never intended to hurt my mother, and the guilt was eating him up.

I saw a softer side of my father, and I even thought about forgiving him, but there are consequences for bullshit. I acted like I forgave him. I had to, my family depended on him for financial support. This opened the door for me to convince him, and have him convince my mom, that it would be okay for me to go visit Justin.

Yes, I played on his emotions. So what? That's life. I knew how to say and do the right thing to get what I wanted.

My father talked it over with my mother. After she thought about it, she decided to allow me to go to Florida. But first, she needed to talk with me.

"Stormi, your father has convinced me that you're old enough to travel and I should trust your judgment, but I still want to hear what you have to say on the matter. You have never been away from home on your own. Are you sure you are going to be okay flying by yourself?"

"Mom, I'm eighteen years old, almost nineteen. It's time for me to spread my wings. Don't worry about me. I'll be okay."

"I understand, but you're going to be gone for the duration of the summer and your dad and I aren't comfortable with you staying at Justin's. We're willing to pay for you to have your own place."

"You'd be wasting your money. I know without a shadow of a doubt that I'll be staying with Justin, and if I allow you to get me a place, it's only to make you feel better. I refuse to let you waste your money. Mom, I know this is a lot to handle, but I'm a big girl and I can take care my-self. I need this break!"

"Stormi, you've dealt with so much tragedy in the last couple of years, and I haven't taken the time to talk with you about the things that make you a woman. Now that you are transitioning from youth to young adult, we need to have a talk. By staying in the same apartment with Justin, you are putting yourself in a position to fornicate. You have to remember you committed yourself to God in your purity class. It's not too late for me to get you your own place. I have already been working on it. Sister Johnson has a sister that lives in Flor-ida. She will rent you a room in her home and you can come and go as you please. I just want to help you make the right decision. You should save yourself for your marriage."

"It's too late for us to have this conversation. I'm not a virgin anymore. I haven't been for a long time. I mean you no disrespect, but I couldn't care less about marriage. I can clearly see that people ain't loyal to one another. Dad cheated on you and even had the nerve to have a kid with her. To top it off, he wants you to consider raising his bastard child. So, you see, I don't have that warm and fuzzy feeling about marriage. I think it's all bull. People do what they want, with whom they want. Nobody understands commitment."

"I feel like I have failed you, Stormi. I've always thought of you as my baby."

"I stopped being your baby a long time ago. Mom, you don't have to worry about me getting pregnant. I've never had sex with Justin. He has always avoided it, so I think he's either a virgin or he's gay. One way or another, I'll find out."

THEY CALL ME STORMI RAIN

13

The Flight from Hell

Several weeks had passed and finally the day arrived for me to leave for Florida. My mother took me to the airport. When we arrived, she wouldn't let go of my hand.

"Mom, I have to go or I'll miss my plane. Don't look so worried. I'll be okay."

Before I got out of the car, I kissed my mother goodbye. As I walked into the airport, I turned to look back at her. I could see the tears running down her face. The last thing I wanted was to hurt my mother.

I walked up to the counter to check my bags and James greeted me. He was dressed in an airline uniform. *I must be dreaming. This can't be happening to me.* He was my first everything. My first boyfriend, my first lover, the first man to lie to me, and the first man to cheat on me. James covered up King raping Shannon. This dude broke my heart into pieces, and now I was standing right in front of him.

He didn't recognize me at first glance; I hadn't seen him in a long time. I kept my head down and gave him my ID without looking up.

He looked at my ID, then at me, and then back at my ID.

"Stormi, is that you? Girl, I can't believe my eyes. I haven't seen you in a while. Wow, you look amazing. You've turned out to be a gorgeous chick. I see you're traveling to Florida."

There was something about James that made my heart go pitter-patter. As a young girl, I would get excited every time I'd see him. I was experiencing some of those same emotions.

It's something about your first love. You never get over them. James made me weak at the knees despite how he treated me. I had that stupid love for him. He could piss on me and I'd still hold a place in my heart for him.

I mustered up enough courage to look him in his eyes and acted as though I didn't know him.

"Sir, can I have my boarding pass and ID please?"

"You don't have to act so professional. We're allowed to interact with the customers. It's really good to see you." James gave my ID a once-over before he handed it back with my boarding pass.

"Stormi, I never knew your actual name. I thought it was just Stormi. Simone Mona Lisa Johnson, that's different."

"Yeah, well, you didn't know my name because you never took the time to get to know me. All you wanted was my jewel box. Who I am as a person meant nothing to you."

"That's not true. I genuinely cared for you. Stormi, let me make it up to you."

I took my boarding pass and ID and headed to the security checkpoint. As I was walking away, I could hear James yelling goodbye.

"Bye, Mona Lisa. I'll be waiting for your return."

I didn't respond to James. I continued up the escalator and went through security.

This was the first time my name had been revealed. No one knew my real name. I hated it. I asked my mother why she would give me such a crazy name. She told me one day I'd appreciate it. She named me Simone after Nina Simone. She was a singer, pianist, civil rights activist, and journalist. She named me Mona Lisa after the portrait by Leonardo da Vinci. She loved Mona Lisa's smile. My mother thought she looked happy, and that's what she wanted for me. She told me once she held me in her arms, she knew it would be the perfect name. Well, I preferred Stormi—my father got it right when he came up with my nickname. The day will come when I'll legally change my name.

As I boarded the plane, I let out a sigh of relief. I was ready to embark upon my new journey. I smiled as I walked down the aisle. It felt great to be traveling by myself for the first time. When I got to my seat, I was excited to see I had the window seat. I sat down, closed my eyes, and took a deep breath. The flight attendant announced we'd be taxiing to the runway, so I buckled up and put a pillow behind my head. The seat next to mine was still empty, and that meant more room for me. Just before the plane was ready to pull from the gate, the captain announced that they were waiting for the last passenger to board. I kept my eyes closed and waited for the plane to take off. The next thing I knew, someone was rubbing my leg. I quickly opened my eyes in a panic. Trent was sitting next to me. My heart started beating fast. I rubbed my eyes to make sure I wasn't dreaming. I wasn't; it was Trent in the flesh.

"What's going on? Why are you here?"

"I should be asking you the same question, Stormi."

"I'm on my way to see Justin."

"Well, I'm on my way to see Justin, too."

"What do you mean?"

"Justin and I spoke several weeks ago and he told me I could make some good money in Florida. He wanted me to come down and visit with him and a couple of his friends. So I bought a ticket."

"Is Justin expecting you?"

"Naw, I thought I'd surprise him."

"I don't believe you. You picked this day. The day I'm going. You've got to be kidding me."

"Stormi, this is a coincidence. Don't get your panties in a bunch. I had no idea you were going to see Justin."

"Wow, this is unbelievable."

"Let's just make the best of it."

I looked out the window and shook my head in disbelief. How was it possible that Trent and I ended up on the same plane going to visit Justin at the same time? It was crazy. As bad as I wanted to ignore him, I couldn't. Hell, I owed him money. Instead, I was determined to find out what kind of business Trent was doing with Justin and why Justin never mentioned it to me. I knew about the steroids, but I thought that was over.

"So, Trent, what type of business are you and Justin doing that requires you to come to Florida?"

"Justin has a lot of new friends with money. He thought it would be a good idea for me to meet them."

"That sounds like some bullshit. Justin's on the straight and narrow. He wouldn't get caught up in some illegal shit with you."

"All he has to do is make the introduction. I'll take care of the rest. We have a long ride ahead of us. Let's enjoy it."

I closed my eyes but couldn't fall asleep. I couldn't believe Justin would get involved with Trent and not tell me. I was hoping this trip would bring Justin and me closer, but I had a feeling it was going to make or break our relationship. I felt like I couldn't trust him anymore.

I finally fell asleep but I kept waking up because the plane was so cold. I nudged Trent and asked him to get me a blanket from the overhead bin. When he got up, I saw him in a different light. I saw someone who genuinely cared for me. Yes, he was rough around the edges, but he was a real man. Trent placed the blanket over me and I fell asleep, but not before he kissed me gently on the forehead.

After being asleep for about an hour, I was awakened by severe turbulence. The seat belt lights were flashing and the flight attendants were telling everyone to remain calm and stay in their seats. The pilot announced we were experiencing an unexpected storm, and he had to dodge it. In order to do that, he had to fly the plane at a higher altitude. As the flight attendants were picking up all liquids and trash, the turbulence became worse. Food and drinks flew all over the place. Some of the luggage from the overhead bins fell out, and several people sitting in their seats were struck in the head. The oxygen masks fell once the pressure changed and we were instructed to put them on.

My heart was beating out of my chest. I became dizzy and couldn't breathe. The abrupt onset of fear pushed me to my breaking point. I was in a full-blown panic attack. I was now reliving every traumatic experience I had encountered in my life.

I saw myself floating in the atmosphere. It was beautiful and serene; the sky was clear and very blue. I was floating among the clouds. I reached out to grab hold of one. I wrapped my arms around it. I was cut. The cloud was a frozen icicle. I tried to let go, but my skin had stuck to the ice. What I thought represented beauty represented pain. As I tried to release myself, I had visions of James pushing his one-eyed snake inside me as he stole my virginity.

I was released only to float to another cloud to see Shannon being raped by King. Another cloud showed me the scene of Shannon hanging from the ceiling fan as she tried to commit suicide. The next one showed the burial of Joy. I fought even harder to get away from that cloud. I drifted away from Joy and I was floating around the atmosphere. I came upon another cloud, but this time I knew it was different. It was double the size and extremely beautiful, so I reached for it. It was soft and fluffy like I had imagined. I knew I was safe. I could feel myself relaxing.

"Bang!" One shot to the head and Shannon was dead. I immediately let go of that cloud. I started falling from the sky, heading straight for the water. As I was falling, I had visions of Derrick lying in the street with blood oozing from his body.

I was going to die in the water. That was my destiny. The devil wasn't allowed to drown me at birth, but he was allowed to torment me. I was under attack. Where was God?

Stormi Rain: You're on your own. You better learn how to swim quickly. If you don't, you're going to drown. God is allowing all these things

to happen to you. You should stop crying out to him for help, he's showing you No Mercy!

The plane hit the water and sank fast. I was underwater, struggling to come up for air. I couldn't swim. I floated to the top. I tried to keep my head above the water, but I would sink right back down. My mouth was open. I had swallowed a lot of water; I was drowning slowly. The current pulled me farther down. I felt death all around me. Before I completely gave into my demise, I saw my mother underwater with me. She was reaching her hand out to save me. I reached for her hand, but I was too far away. I drifted farther away from her. The sea was taking me away; I was floating into the darkness. I then saw a beam of light. I could see Shannon floating toward me. She was motioning for me to grab her hand. My body floated to her. I was almost in her reach; my fingertips were touching hers. Before Shannon could completely grab my hand, my mother floated between us, grabbed my hand, and pulled me away. My mother shook her head, saying no to Shannon, and she floated away.

Trent quickly pulled me close to him and assisted me with putting on my oxygen mask. He held my hand and told me not to worry. The plane reached a normal altitude and we were able to take off the oxygen masks. My breathing returned to normal and I calmed down. I was grateful that Trent and I were on the same flight; if he hadn't been, I would've died from fear.

"Stormi, are you okay?"

"Yes, I'm okay, but you have no idea what I just relived. My mind was playing tricks on me."

"Do you need anything? I thought you were unconscious, I kept calling your name and you wouldn't respond. Then all of a sudden, you opened your eyes and I was able to help you put on your oxygen mask."

"Trent, I don't know what happened. It was like I was in a dream. I don't know what I would've done if you hadn't been here."

"No worries, I won't let anything happen to you. We'll be landing soon. I want you to relax."

I held Trent's hand for the duration of the flight. He was strong and confident and he helped me through my panic attack. He knew just what to do to calm me down and didn't judge me. The pilot announced we'd be on the ground in the next five minutes and apologized for the turbulence we experienced.

Once the plane landed, we exited and Trent and I went our separate ways.

THEY CALL ME STORMI RAIN

14

FLORIDA

As I reached for my luggage on the carousel, I heard someone say, "Baby got backs."

When I turned to see who it was, I was surprised to see Justin. He grabbed me, kissed me, and held me tight. I was in shock. This wasn't the Justin I knew. He was actually showing affection in public.

Wow, things have changed.

"Stormi, I'm glad you're here. I can't wait to show you around."

Justin was always so serious. His focus was always on school, so this kind of welcome could only mean one thing: I'm going to have a good time in Florida.

"Justin, I'm super excited to be here, but I just got off the flight from hell. It was horrible."

"Let's get your luggage and you can tell me all about your flight on the ride home."

As we walked to Justin's car, I thought about Trent and the horrific airplane ride. He held it together and made me feel safe. I was grateful. Justin opened the car door for me and put my bags in the trunk. He was very talkative, which was unusual. We didn't discuss my plane ride like he said we would.

I tried to be a good listener, but my mind drifted off with thoughts of Trent. My plans were to speak with Justin about their business deal, but after what I had just gone through, I decided to hold my tongue.

The first stop was his apartment; it was a nice two-bedroom with a large living room and two bathrooms. I was impressed. I put my bags in his bedroom and toured the rest of the apartment. When I tried to look in the other bedroom, the door was locked. Justin informed me that he had a roommate, but it didn't work out between them. He left some of his things and would be coming back to get them.

Justin appeared to be doing well for himself. He told me to freshen up so he could take me on a tour of the university. I just wanted to lie down and gather my thoughts. I asked Justin to give me an hour. I needed to take a shower and pull myself together. The bathroom had always been my sanctuary. I would take long, hot baths or showers and it would always make me feel better. I had done some of my best thinking in the shower.

I turned on the shower. The water was hot and steamed up the bathroom quickly. The hot water relaxed my tense body. When I held my head back to let the water run on my face, I realized I didn't have a shower cap on. I jumped out the shower and ran into the bedroom butt ass naked to get it out of my luggage. There was no way I was going to get my newly straightened hair wet. Though, my natural curly locks would do.

I jumped back into the shower. It refreshed me and I was able to put on my happy face. My energy was back and I was ready to roll.

As we drove to the university, I rolled the window down to take in the fresh air. We arrived on campus and Justin showed me every inch of it. He was excited about his school, and it was very impressive.

Once we left, he took me to a beautiful restaurant on the beach. I was famished. Justin pulled my chair out and we sat down. The waiter gave us menus to look over, but it was obvious that Justin already knew what he wanted. He told me he had been there before, so if I didn't mind, he'd like to order for me. Of course I didn't mind; I was new to all of this, so he actually helped me out. When the waiter approached, Justin ordered our food, and to my surprise, an alcoholic beverage. I decided to go with the flow and just see what would happen. The waiter brought us a margarita. It was my first alcoholic drink and I got to share it with Justin.

"Justin, this is a beautiful restaurant. I'm surprised they didn't ask you for ID."

"I come here a lot. Not once has anyone ever asked me for ID. But even if they did, I have a fake one."

"Yeah, but what if they would have asked for mine?"

"Stormi, I have you covered. I had a friend of mine make you one as well."

"Wow, Justin, you've changed."

"You would be amazed at how fast you can adapt to college life. There's so much to learn and so much to do. I've been having a great time. That's why I decided to stay and go to summer school. This has been a great opportunity for me and I'm having the time of my life."

"Who pays for all your living expenses?"

"I have a grant that covers it."

"That's great, Justin. Your grant covers the summer school program as well?"

"No, I have to cover that myself."

"I'm sure it's expensive for your parents."

"Stormi, my parents don't have the money to cover this. I have a side hustle that covers my expenses."

"Oh, I understand. You have to do what you have to do."

I was well aware that sometimes you have to hustle to get what you need. Justin had to handle his business and I understood.

After a long day, Justin and I headed back to his apartment to get some rest. Justin informed me we had been invited to a party. I was tired from traveling and running around Florida, so I wanted to tell Justin I didn't want to go, but I didn't want to be a party pooper. Justin was being attentive to my every need. He helped me unpack my bags and ran me a hot bubble bath. I was excited. We had never been alone like this before, and we were free to do whatever we wanted.

"Stormi your bath is ready. Take your time and relax. Once you're done, take a nap and get some rest. I'll wake you when it's time for you to get dressed."

"You're not going to join me?'

"No, I have some business I need to handle."

I stood in the middle of the bathroom floor staring at myself in the mirror. I took my clothes off slowly, hoping that Justin would come in, see my naked body, go crazy, and make love to me for the first time. My body had developed nicely. My breasts were like sweet peaches and my ass was round and firm. Things had changed for me. I was no longer that insecure little girl anymore. When I looked in the mirror, I didn't see my flaws. I saw my assets.

I held my breasts in my hands and gave them a little jiggle and then I rubbed my ass. Yes, it was time to get my jewel box tuned up. The last man that made love to me was Trent, and I almost told him I loved him. I had to get myself together after that encounter. He was amazing. The only other person that had touched my jewel box in such a way was Bryce with his lips.

I wanted Justin to make love to me, so I called him back into the bathroom while I stood naked.

Justin entered and stared at me with desire in his eyes. That's the response I wanted; he had never seen me naked. My jewel box was shaved just right. I had gotten good at it over the years. I even started shaving a lightning bolt in my pubic hairs as a reminder of my storms.

Justin walked over to me and turned me around so my back was facing him. He blew his hot breath on my neck and made his way down my spine. I was squirming like a snake anticipating his next move.

He whispered in my ear, "Enjoy your bath," and walked out the door.

Justin remained a gentleman.

THEY CALL ME STORMI RAIN

15

The Party

We walked into the party and everyone greeted Justin as if he were a celebrity. "Fantastic Voyage" by Lakeside was playing. Justin grabbed my hand and we hit the dance floor. We danced for the entire song and then the DJ put on "Square Biz" by Tina Marie. We were having a great time.

Justin was the life of the party; I had never seen him in this light before. He was easy-going and enjoyed the simple things in life. It was obvious things had changed since he arrived in Florida.

It was apparent that the female students had taken notice of Justin—all eyes were on him. Several girls walked up to him while we were dancing and gave him a kiss. I acted as if it didn't bother me, but it did.

Stormi Rain: It appears your little boyfriend has fans. You lay low and don't say a word. All you have to do is give them that "I'm a boss chick" look. The kisses will stop. If they don't, we'll handle our business.

After dancing through two records straight, I wanted to sit down. Justin told me he was going to mingle with some of his friends and he'd be right back to check on me.

I watched how Justin worked the room. He had so much energy. You would've thought he was the host. I was amazed at how many people he had gotten to know in such a small amount of time. He talked with almost everyone in the room, drink in hand. I sat patiently waiting for his return.

Justin came over to the couch and took a seat next to me. We sat holding hands and kissing. Justin's female friends made their way over to us. One of them kept leaning over and whispering in his ear. I gave her that "If you don't leave him alone, I'm going to beat your ass" look. She acted as if she didn't care. She continued to flirt with him, daring me to say something. I was itching to, but I didn't want to appear jealous. I acted as if her presence wasn't a problem. Justin whispered in my ear that he needed to handle some business. When he got up to leave, so did the girl that was whispering in his ear and the other groupies.

This didn't sit well with me, but there was nothing I could do about it. I just kept a watchful eye on them. They entered a room I saw several other people visit frequently. It was obvious this room was only for an exclusive group of people.

As I waited for Justin, my mind ran wild thinking of all the things that could be going on in there. I tried to keep myself calm and not let my imagination take over. After waiting for well over forty minutes, I knew it was time for me to get up and find him. Someone was coming out of the room, so I held the door open with my foot to peek in. I couldn't believe my eyes. Trent and Justin were sitting at a table together conducting drug transactions. There was a table full of cocaine and money. People were standing in line. They'd give Justin the money, Trent would hand them a short straw, and they'd lean over and snort a line of coke. I wasn't familiar with this drug, but I knew it was Trent's new money-maker he told me about. I watched Justin collect the money and from time to time, he would stick his finger in the white powder and rub it on his gums. I couldn't understand why Justin was jeopardizing his future by letting Trent pimp him. If the police were to raid this place and Justin was in possession of all that money, he'd be considered the dealer, not Trent. Trent taught me that. He would always say, "Baby girl, never get your hands dirty. Let someone else handle the money and the product if you can. If you were ever raided, nothing would be in your possession. You would be considered a user, and users don't do time."

I retreated to the couch to gather my thoughts. I was feeling betrayed by both of them. I was thinking about my next move when Justin appeared in front of me.

"Justin, what's going on? Damn, I've been sitting here for forty minutes waiting on you."

"I'm sorry, I got caught up talking about sports with some of the fellas. I didn't realize I was gone that long."

"It's okay. I just felt out of place."

"No need to feel that way. You'll soon be attending school here. It takes time to adjust. I felt strange at first, too. It's nothing like high school."

"You can say that again."

"Come on, Stormi, let's go home. I'm getting tired."

Did he say he was getting tired? He had to be kidding me. He ran around this party all night acting like a kid on a sugar high, now all of a sudden he was tired? I guess he was crashing from being high on coke.

The drive home was quiet. I wanted to say something about his business with Trent, but I decided to wait and let him tell me when he was ready. We arrived at Justin's apartment, and as soon as he opened the door for me, I could see rose petals on the floor.

I immediately turned and wrapped my arms around him. I was blown away. He guided me to the bathroom where there was a rose petal bath with candles waiting for me.

I was at a loss for words. I had been waiting for this moment. Justin began to undress me. Every time he removed a piece of my clothing, my body would shake. When he got to the last piece, I was standing naked looking at him.

"Stormi, I know you've been waiting for this for a long time. I wanted it to be just right for you. The girls at the party set this up for me. I know you thought something else was going on, but it wasn't. I want you to know you're the girl of my dreams. I love you. I'm working on building a future for us. I want to be the man you deserve. I knew when I first met you that you'd be mine. It doesn't matter about your past because I'm your future. I have our lives all planned out. Four years from now, you'll be my wife. I'll cherish you and love you like no other. Just know that I have always put you first and everything I do is for you. I just have one question."

Justin got on his knees while I stood naked with tears streaming down my face.

"Simone Mona Lisa Johnson, will you marry me in four years?"

Without hesitation, I said, "Yes."

Justin opened the medicine cabinet and retrieved a jewelry box. I couldn't believe my eyes, he opened the box and there was a beautiful diamond ring inside. He placed it on my finger and it fit perfectly. I became weak in the knees. The thought of becoming Justin's wife was unbelievable. I was astonished that he had planned this far ahead. Everything about his proposal was amazing. I really didn't know what to do. Justin held my hand and helped me over into the tub. I got in and immediately immersed my full body under the water. When I came up, I could see Justin standing naked. His body was abnormally fine. He had muscles in all the right places. His chest was chiseled and his abs were tighter than mine. He ran track, so his legs looked like they belonged to a Greek god. I knew it was going to be a long night. Oh my, I forgot my shower cap!

THEY CALL ME STORMI RAIN

Six Months Later

16

EVERYTHING APPEARED TO BE PERFECT

It had been a long, hard six months, but soon all my hard work in community college would pay off. All my credits were transferable and I'd be attending Florida State University next fall as a sophomore. I had to make sure I didn't deviate from the plan Justin had put in place. I would soon be with him on a full-time basis and he and I would graduate together.

I was in awe of Justin. Everything about him had changed. I really appreciated the time and effort he put into our relationship. Justin would fly me to Florida every other month to keep our love alive. He didn't believe that absence made the heart grow fonder. Truth be told, I thought he was just a control freak, or he just didn't trust me. Whatever the case, I enjoyed seeing him every other month.

Everything appeared to be perfect. Derrick had made a full recovery. The specialist did a great job on rehabilitating him. Gabby had been released from the crazy house and was now part of my money team. At first, I wasn't sure if she was stable enough to work. She would work for a couple of weeks and then disappear and no one would hear from her for days. This went on for several weeks. Her mother had convinced her not to press charges against Juan and to admit she was lying about the molestation.

She loved her mother so much she agreed to it. She thought it would make the relationship between her and her mother stronger. She promised Gabby she'd put Juan out of their house and Gabby could come home.

Gabby's first weeks home were great. Gabby was like a new person. She was excited to be home and it appeared her mother had done what she had promised. Juan was no longer living in the house. I would visit on occasion. When Gabby started making money, her mother was the first to reap the benefits. She never asked any questions as far as where Gabby got the money. She just happily took it.

One night while Gabby was sleeping, she heard some noise coming from her mother's room. She got out of bed and knocked on her mother's door to make sure she was okay. She didn't answer. She continued to bang on the door. She heard voices coming from her mother's room.

She pressed her ear against the door and could hear Juan's voice. Gabby heard him tell her mother that he refused to keep hiding from Gabby's fat ass and if she still wanted to be with him, she had better tell her he was moving back in the house.

Gabby listened to her mother beg Juan not to leave. She told Juan that Gabby was helping with her bills, and as soon as she got the last of her bills paid, she would put Gabby out. Then he'd be able to move back in. Juan made it clear that he didn't care about her bills, she needed to choose between him and Gabby right now. Gabby continued to listen with tears running down her face, remaining hopeful that her mother would choose her. Before she could hear her mother's answer, she decided to pack her bags and leave.

That night, Gabby moved in with her grandmother, YaYa. She vowed never to speak to her mother again. She wanted to start her life over.

YaYa loved Gabby and knew she was telling the truth about Juan. She welcomed her with open arms. Gabby's grandmother was a prayer warrior. She would always tell Gabby she needed to trust in God and everything would work out. She explained that the only way she'd be free is if she forgave Juan and her mother. Gabby's heart was broken that her mother chose Juan over her, but it wasn't the first time. Gabby's mother didn't love her and she knew it, but the need for her mother's love was stronger than her reality. She'd get depressed and leave for days at a time.

YaYa would drive around searching for Gabby. When she would find her, she'd bring her back home and nurse her emotional health with prayer and worship. Her last episode was bad. YaYa reached out to a priest she knew and they performed an exorcism on Gabby.

I went to visit Gabby and she appeared to be doing well. During my visit, YaYa told me she needed to pray over me. She wanted to make sure I wasn't an evil spirit. I didn't want to be rude, so I allowed her to, even though I thought it was nonsense. She told me she saw a dark cloud around me, but that God was still protecting me. I thought to myself, *this woman is crazy*. I wanted to tell her the so-called dark cloud she saw was the blackness of my heart.

YaYa gave Gabby and me rosary beads. She told us to keep them with us at all times. I went along with it because Gabby needed me to; she swore by the beads. She believed they kept her safe. She became obsessed with prayer. She prayed about everything. She even prayed she'd have good dope sales…and she did.

Juan had been gone for several months. He just up and disappeared. He left everything he owned behind. It was as if he fell off the face of the earth. Gabby believed it was the power of the beads. I, on the other hand, believed Trent had something to do with Juan's disappearance.

Five months ago, while dropping off a payment to Trent, we did our usual. We sat and talked about business and life in general. The experience from the flight from hell made Trent and me great friends. Once we returned home from Florida, we never spoke about his business venture with Justin. He didn't even know I saw him in the room.

Trent became my confidant. We talked about everything. I could tell him my most private secrets. He was my best male friend. He'd give me advice on my relationship with Justin, and help me with whatever I needed—no strings attached. I felt free to be myself with him.

When Gabby was released, I had a conversation with Trent about her being on my money team. I wanted to know if he thought it'd be a good idea. The fact that we both had been treated for mental illness was a concern. There would be no need to have two people going cuckoo for cocoa puffs in the streets. I told him about Gabby being molested by her mother's boyfriend at the age of ten. As I told him her story, he began to look off into space. I asked him if he was okay; he insisted that I continue.

I told him about the gruesome rape she suffered and the mental trauma she lives with every day. Trent became enraged and began to pace the floor.

Trent wanted to know where Juan lived, where he worked, and where he hung out. He wanted his phone number, too. I questioned his need for this information. I asked him what was going on, and he told me his stepfather raped his sister when she was ten. He walked in on him raping her, and when Trent tried to get him off her, he punched Trent in the face and threw him to the ground. Trent got up and ran into the kitchen to get a knife.

He walked back into the room where his stepfa-ther was still raping his sister. He held the knife up in the air with both hands. He closed his eyes and stabbed him several times in his back. His stepfather fell off his sister and onto the floor. Trent called 911 and ran to his sister's aid. She was lying on the floor dead with her eyes wide open. When the police and paramedics arrived, his sister was pronounced dead at the scene. His step-father is serving a life sentence.

When Gabby first told me Juan was gone, I didn't think anything of it. But as time passed, her mother became worried and started putting up missing person's flyers. Gabby told her mother she was wasting her time searching for him.

Gabby told her she prayed him away, and there was no way he was coming back. Gabby's mother thought someone reported him to Immigration. Juan was here illegally, so it didn't matter that he was missing. I asked Trent if he had anything to do with his disappearance.

His response was, "How's Gabby doing?"

Gabby's now in her happy place and thriving. She's hustling her ass off. When I leave, I'm going to leave my operation in her hands.

I know I should give it up completely, and I will, as soon as I graduate college. For now, I'm going to need the money to make it through school. I refuse to put a financial burden on my parents.

I'm two payments shy of paying off my loan from Trent.

THEY CALL ME STORMI RAIN

17

THINGS WERE LOOKING UP

Things were looking up for me. I was now able to control the bad thoughts that once controlled me. The depression, the lack of self-worth, and the feelings of brokenness were all gone. I finally felt I was good enough to move forward in life. I was well on my way to a happy life with Justin.

The thought of living in a different state where no one knew me was exciting. I could actually start over. All the bad memories would be gone.

At times, I'd get sad at the thought of not being here for my sisters. They were maturing fast…but not that fast. Well, one thing's for sure, I wouldn't have to worry about King's dog ass coming in contact with them. King was incarcerated. He became strung out on a new drug that had been introduced to the neighborhood called crack. He tried to rob a liquor store to support his habit and was caught.

Crack is the crystal form of cocaine. It's heated and smoked, and it's far stronger and more potent than regular cocaine. It was the poor man's high. It made people do unthinkable things. I stuck with selling weed. Trent and his snow bunny dealt with that heavy stuff.

Stormi Rain: Maybe it's just good luck, but something or someone is helping us with our hit list. That motherfucka King has been handled. The drugs have destroyed his mind and now he's incarcerated. Maybe someone will rape him like

he raped Shannon. That bitch Babette is incarnated for life. She's now out of your mother's way. However, her son may still be a problem. Well, we for sure won't do anything to a little kid. Nevertheless, we can make Babette believe we will. That's what you call mental torture.

Juan's sucio culo (dirty ass) is gone and nowhere to be found. That makes Gabby's life easier. We have James and Reese left to handle. Oh, yeah, and I was thinking we should get the nurse that gave Joy the wrong medicine.

Someone else is doing our job and having all the fun. You need to get your head in the game. We don't have time to waste. You're putting all your energy into going to school. We need to finish what we started. Remember you vowed No Mercy.

I had been trying to prepare my mother for my big move. Even though it was over six months away, I still felt like I needed to prepare her early.

I tried to have conversations about it, but she'd change the subject.

I believed it was her way of coping; she wasn't ready to let go of me. I understood how she felt. My track record on handling tragedy wasn't that great. I knew she'd be concerned with me being so far away and the possibility of me having another breakdown.

I didn't want my mother to worry about me. She had other things to deal with. My father was still hoping she would agree to his bastard son coming to live with us. That was a lot all by itself. I often wondered how he would feel if my mother had an affair and it resulted in a pregnancy. I know he wouldn't allow her to bring another man's child into our home, so why would he expect her to allow him to bring his? He was asking way too much of her.

I could hear my mother saying, "Philippians 4:13 says, 'I can do all things through Christ who strengthens me.' All my help comes from the Lord. He will guide my footsteps."

I just hoped he wouldn't guide her to mother a child she didn't give birth to.

———— ♦ ————

I had so much on my plate and my mind was all over the place. I was trying hard to stay motivated. It would soon be time for me to visit Justin. I needed to pull myself together so I could remain focused. Justin had worked hard on planning our life together. I didn't want him to think I wasn't ready for our journey. Visiting Justin always made me happy.

I needed advice on how to get my mother to accept that I'd be going away for school. Trent was a good listener and had always given me good, sound advice. I thought it would be a good idea to pay him a visit.

I called to see if it was okay to stop by. Trent had made a lot of money with the sale of crack. He now owned several new cars and his wardrobe was out of this world. He wore nothing but name brand—Gucci, Louis Vuitton, just to name a few. He wore a custom-made diamond cross. It was amazing to look at. I had never seen so many diamonds.

I never understood why drug dealers or other unscrupulous people always tried to protect themselves by wearing a cross. It didn't make sense to me.

Trent moved to an upscale neighborhood. He was no longer down the street. He was now up the hill. These were Trent's words to live by. *"Never lay your head where you do business."*

I had been to Trent's new place (palace) on several occasions, but each time felt like a new adventure. To get to Trent's house, you had to travel up a private, winding road. There were several other houses in the neighborhood, but each one had its own long driveway leading to the property. None of the houses were within walking distance of each other.

My father had done construction work on some of the homes in Trent's neighborhood. I was well aware of what it costs to live there. Trent told me I could live the same lifestyle if I wanted to. I couldn't see myself hustling my entire life. In order to live in that manner, you'd have to sell a lot of crack, and I wasn't willing. Crack was changing people's lives. If you were caught selling crack, you could receive a life prison sentence, even though it's a nonviolent offense.

I wasn't prepared to give up my life. They say don't do the crime if you can't do the time. My small weed operation would get me an insignificant punishment, and that was all I was willing to risk. I had money saved. If I wanted to, I could drive a fancy car, but too many questions would be asked. I stuck with driving the Chevy Chevette that my parents had purchased for me when I graduated high school. I was grateful for what I had. I knew better than to push the limits.

Malcolm X stated, *"Without education, you are not going anywhere in this world."* I knew that no matter what type of business I was in, I needed to be educated—even if it was the dope business. I told Trent once I graduated from college, I was going to help him become legit. The risk of selling drugs was too high. He needed to invest so he wouldn't have to maintain his lifestyle by selling crack.

I had been driving for about thirty minutes. I finally made it to Trent's house, or what I called his mini mansion. My underarms began to sweat just walking from his circular driveway to his double doors. I thought the number of stairs I had to climb was ridiculous, but far be it for me to complain.

I rang the doorbell and waited for Trent to answer. He opened the door with a big ol' smile on his face.

"Hey, baby girl, how you doing?"

"Trent, I need some water. I feel like I just took a hike to get to your front door."

"Girl, come on in. You can have whatever you like. You know your way to the kitchen. Help yourself."

I walked to the kitchen to get some water and followed Trent outside to his patio. He gave me a great big hug and kiss on the cheek.

Trent and I have not been involved sexually for quite some time now. Our friendship was more important to us. We didn't want to jeopardize the love we shared as friends. Jessica was his new love and I had grown accustomed to that. She was a down ass chick, to say the least. The things she was willing to do for love and money were beyond me.

"Baby girl, it's good to see you. How's business?"

"Business is good, I'm actually feeling good about the direction my life is headed."

"That's what up."

"I've been trying to get my mother to accept that I'll be moving to Florida for school."

"Is that right? I thought you had changed your mind about moving to Florida."

"What? Why would you think that? I've been working my ass off going to community college."

"Well, you stopped talking about school. I figured you were okay with going to school here. I told you I'd help in any way I could financially."

"I know, Trent, but I need a change. Derrick's doing great. He's back on his feet, thanks to you. I want to be with Justin. Before Derrick was shot, we had made plans to go to school together and graduate with our degrees. Everything is moving in the right direction. I just need my mother to get on board with my plan. That's why I'm here. I need to talk to you about something."

"What's up, baby girl?"

"I'm so excited I can barely contain myself. You remember about six months ago when we both went to Florida to see Justin?"

"Yes, I remember."

"Justin asked me to marry him."

"He did what?" Trent responded in an extremely loud voice.

"Why are you shouting?"

"Baby girl, I'm sorry. That just threw me for a loop."

"Yeah, it threw me for a loop, too."

"Did you accept his proposal?"

"Yes, I did. That's why I've been working so hard. We have a plan in place."

There was a long silence. Trent was looking off into space. It appeared he wasn't paying attention to what I was saying.

"Trent, did you hear what I just said?"

"Yes, I heard you. I'm processing. You know, Stormi, I think you're too young to get married. You have your entire life ahead of you. Justin might not be the right guy for you."

"What? Trent, I thought you liked Justin. You even went into business with him. What are you saying?"

"I think you should slow down. I feel like you're moving too fast."

"Wow, I didn't expect this from you. I thought you were on my side."

Trent started rubbing his head as if he had a headache.

"Trent, are you okay?"

"Yes, I'm okay. Excuse me, I going to go and get us some hash. I need to smoke. I'll be right back."

"Okay."

Trent excused himself. I was surprised at his response. I thought he'd be excited for me. I was hoping he'd tell me how to break the news to my parents. He didn't even give me enough time to tell him we were going to wait until we finished school.

Thirty minutes had passed and Trent hadn't come back. I could hear him talking on the phone. I decided I wasn't going to wait any longer. I got up to get the hashish. As I approached his room, I could hear his conversation. He was telling some-one to stop providing product to one of his Florida connects. Based on what I could interpret from the conversation, the person Trent was speaking with was trying to get Trent to change his mind.

I heard Trent say, "I don't care how much money they are making. We will no longer supply them. I have been betrayed."

I hesitated before I walked into his room. It appeared he had several people working for him in Florida. Maybe a crewmember was keeping more than their fair share of the proceeds. Hell, for all I knew, he could have been talking about Justin. I was hoping Justin wasn't in too deep with Trent. When you first start making money, it becomes addictive—you don't want to stop.

I felt sorry for whoever the dealer was. It's hard when you get kicked out of the game. No one else will work with you. If you haven't saved any money, you end up broke.

I never questioned Justin and Trent's relationship. I had decided to stay out of it. It's not good for a relationship when your girl is in all your business.

I decided to let Justin be his own man. If he wanted to work with Trent, that was his business. I walked into Trent's humongous bedroom and took the hash out of his hands while he was talking on the phone. I went and sat by the pool, kicked my feet up, and got high as a kite.

THEY CALL ME STORMI RAIN

18

SEVEN WHOLE DAYS

It was time for my daily phone call with Justin. He and I spoke on the phone like clockwork. Justin was anal when it came to time management. He would always say, "Time is money." So when he missed our first phone call, I got a little uneasy. It wasn't like him. I figured he was catching up on his schoolwork. He had been studying extremely hard. He wanted to make the dean's list. Then he missed the second, third, fourth, fifth, and sixth call. Before I knew it, seven days had passed without a word from Justin.

I was out of my mind with worry. I didn't know what to do, but I knew I had to do something. I decided I would visit his parents.

My mind was running wild. I thought of him lying in a ditch somewhere, hurt. I had a dream that he had met someone new and wasn't interested in me anymore. I didn't know what to think.

Justin's parents lived about twenty minutes away. I got into my car and headed to their house. While driving "All I Do Is Think of You" by Troop was playing on the radio.

The music was speaking to my heart. My tears began to flow.

I pulled over and looked in my glove compartment for a napkin to wipe my face. I got out the car to get some air. I paced back and forth, taking deep breaths.

Stormi Rain: Pull yourself together and get off the emotional rollercoaster. In this game of life, sometimes you win and sometimes you lose.

I got back into the car and continued to Justin's parents' house.

I pulled into their driveway and, before I could even get out of the car, Justin's mother was already walking out of her front door.

"Hello, Stormi. To what do I owe this visit?"

"Hello, I'm sorry for coming by unannounced, but I haven't heard from Justin. I wanted to know if you've heard from him."

"Well, I talked to him two days ago. He was in a bad mood. He was stressed about school. Justin hadn't received his grant money and needed to pay his rent. He didn't want to ask us for the money. You know, he prides himself on being able to handle his own finances. His father and I sent him the money to take care of it. That's probably why you haven't heard from him. I wouldn't worry, dear, he's okay. I'm sure you'll hear from him soon."

"Thank you. I'll wait for him to call. I'm glad to know he's okay."

I started my car and backed out of the driveway. I was more determined than ever to figure out what was going on. Justin had already paid his rent for the whole year. Actually, he had paid all his bills in advance.

Something was going on, and I was going to get to the bottom of it. I headed home to pack my bag. I would be on the first flight to Florida tomorrow morning. I had the ticket that Justin had purchased for my bi-monthly visit, but it was for next week. I would have to pay the difference for using it early.

On my way home, I decided to stop by Trent's house. Maybe he could make sense of what was happening. On my way to his house, it started getting dark. I became apprehensive about driving up the hill, but I kept going anyway. I needed to talk with him. I was stressed. I didn't want to take my anxiety meds because they made me sleepy. If I could just talk to Trent, he'd help me stop spinning out of control. When I arrived, it appeared he had company. I knew I should've called before I stopped by, but it was too late. I walked up the stairs and rang the doorbell. Jessica answered wearing barely anything at all. She had a big smile on her face as she ushered me in. I hurried to pull myself together. There was no way I'd let her see me upset.

As I walked out to the patio, I could hear music playing and smell meat cooking. I saw Trent standing in front of the grill, turning over some steaks.

"Hello."

Trent stood there in silence for a moment. I knew he heard me, but he didn't turn around.

"Trent."

Trent turned around and looked surprised to see me. "Baby girl, what's up?"

"Trent, I really need to talk with you, it's urgent."

"Okay, let's go to my office."

As we headed to Trent's office, I could feel Jessica staring, burning a hole in the back of my head. I turned and looked back at her. The big smile she once wore on her face was no longer there. She was still insecure when it came to Trent and me, as she should be.

When we walked into Trent's office, he closed the door. I fell into Trent's arms. He didn't say a word. He just held me tight as my tears began to flow. He gave me some tissue to dry my eyes. He had already seen me at my worse, so I knew I could trust him with my feelings.

Trent gently raised my head and looked into my eyes. "What's wrong?"

I could barely speak. I wanted him to hold me a little longer. I was concerned about Justin, and I knew he could help me cope with what I was going through.

"Baby girl, tell me what's wrong. I can't help you if you don't tell me."

"I haven't spoken with Justin in seven days. I know something's wrong. I spoke with his mother and she told me she sent him rent money two days ago. I know he paid his rent for the entire year."

"Slow down, everything's going to be okay. If his mother has been in contact with him, he's probably fine."

"Trent, I know for sure something's wrong. Justin and I speak to each other every day. This is totally out of character for him. Are you still doing business with him?"

"Not really, but I did hook him up with a Florida connect."

"Why did you do that?"

"It became harder to supply him with product. I wasn't willing to take the risk of getting caught for drug trafficking."

"Oh, I can understand that."

"I can make some phone calls and see if anyone has seen him, if you want me to."

"That would help. I can't take it anymore, not knowing what's going on. I'm losing sleep over this."

"Baby girl, are you sure you want me to do this? Sometimes people don't want to be found. Maybe he's having a hard time with school and doesn't want to talk to you about it."

"He tells me everything. He loves me with his heart and soul, and I know there's no way in hell he'd just ignore me. I'm leaving on the first flight out in the morning. I know he needs me. I can feel it in my bones. I'm going to find my man. I'm his ride or die chick. I'll call you when I get to Florida and hopefully, you'll have information that can help me find him."

THEY CALL ME STORMI RAIN

19

I Gotta Find My Man

Once I arrived in Florida, I had to figure out how I was going to get to Justin's apartment. I called him when I arrived, but there was no answer. I made my way to the curb to flag a taxi. I didn't have much luggage. I gave the driver the address and I was on my way. I had arrived in Florida around noon, so the traffic was great. I made it to Justin's in about twenty-five minutes. I got out of the taxi, paid the driver,

and walked up to Justin's door. I rang the doorbell, but no answer. I walked to the front of the
apartment building to the manager's office. I met
her on my first visit to Florida; Justin told her I
was his fiancé. I walked into the office and she
greeted me with a smile. I told her I had arrived
earlier than expected, and Justin was still at
school. She handed me the key with no problem.
I headed back to his apartment.

I put the key in the door and turned the knob. I
opened the door slowly and walked in. There were
six TVs sitting in the middle of the floor. I left the
door partially opened, in case I had to run out. I
put my bag down and walked into Justin's bedroom. Everything appeared to be in place. I
walked into the bathroom and found dirty clothes
on the floor. The walls of the shower were still
wet. That was a hopeful sign. To my surprise, the
door to the second bedroom was open. I walked in
and saw several shotguns on the bed. I couldn't

believe my eyes. I immediately became frightened. I stood still for a moment before regaining my composure. This led me to search the dresser drawers. They were empty. I opened the closet to find stacks of jeans with tags still on them. I stood there, puzzled. I felt like I didn't know Justin at all. Things had gotten out of hand. It was obvious he didn't know the first rule of hustling.

"Never house your merchandise where you lay your head."

Storm Rain: You thought because he was smart he would lead you to the promise land. Well, as you can see, he's a fool. He knows nothing about hustling.

I had been staying up for hours at time worrying about Justin's whereabouts. I was irritated from not getting enough sleep. I decided to take a long, hot shower and wait for him to come home. First, I had to give Trent a call. I needed to know if he had any information for me.

I dialed his number. After the sixth ring I decided to hang up, but as I was putting the phone back on the base, I heard someone say, "Hello?"

"Hey, Trent, it's me, Stormi. Did you get any information on Justin?"

"Hey, baby girl, how was your flight? I know you get nervous when you have to fly."

"My flight was fine. I don't mean to rush you, but did you get any information on Justin?"

"Yeah, my boy told me he's still hanging out on the streets. Word is, he owes his connect. He's been trying to hustle up the money to pay them back."

"What the fuck are you talking about?"

"I'm talking about your boy fucked off the money. He has twenty-four hours to make it right, or they goin' shoot his ass."

"I can't believe Justin would take dope from his connect and not pay them."

"Well, he did, and now his ass is in over his head."

"What are you going to do to help him? I feel like you're responsible in a way."

"Look, I showed your boy how to run his business. He knew what he was doing. He got caught up and fucked off the money. How can you blame me for that?"

"Whatever, Trent. I know you, and I'm sure you can make this go away. You're the reason Justin got into the game. You knew he was green and wasn't ready for this lifestyle. How much money does he owe these people?"

"I didn't get a number, but it's enough for those fools to make a move on him."

"Is that right? Well, I guess I better find me some heat for these motherfuckas."

"You've got to be kidding me. You're willing to put in work for him?"

"Hell yeah, I'm going to ride for him. Yo ass acting all nonchalant. You introduced him to the game, and now you're acting like you don't give a damn that he's in trouble."

"It's like that, baby girl? You're willing to ride for Justin? You have no idea who you're going up against."

"I'm his ride or die chick. That's my dude. I'm going to ride for him. There will be no mercy for those that fuck with him."

Stormi Rain: You've got to be kidding me. You're not Bonnie, and he's definitely not Clyde. You need to go home.

"Stormi, you're not ready for this. It's too much at stake. These dudes aren't playing around. They will make you bow down."

"Then make the call and find out how much he owes. Buy me some time so I don't have to bow down."

I was blown away by Trent's response to the situation. I expected more from him. Justin turned him on to the college scene. I'm sure Trent made plenty of money with him. He owed it to Justin to help him out of this mess.

Trent assured me he would make the call. Justin definitely needed my help. I wished he had confided in me before it got to this point. I was tired. The stress had taken a toll on my body. I needed to lie down and take a nap, but I was afraid to go to sleep. I needed a weapon, just in case someone broke into the apartment looking for Justin. I walked into the spare bedroom and picked up a shotgun off the bed. I wasn't familiar with guns at all. I gave it a once-over and decided I better put it down before I shoot myself.

I searched the closet looking for something else to protect myself with. I didn't find anything, so I grabbed a knife out of the kitchen. I hid it under the armrest on the couch. I put my feet up on the coffee table, sat back, and relaxed.

I must have fallen asleep because I was frightened by the turning of the doorknob. I jumped up and grabbed the knife. I was ready to stab someone if I had to. I knew my instinct would be to stab first and ask questions later. I had to be careful. It could be Justin coming through the door.

"Justin, is that you?"

"Yeah."

Justin walked through the door. I couldn't believe my eyes. My handsome, muscular guy looked like a real bum. He was unshaven and it appeared he hadn't had a haircut in a while. This wasn't like him. He was always particular about his appearance. Damn! My heart skipped a beat.

"Stormi, what are you doing here? I wasn't expecting you until next week."

"Justin, it's been damn near a week since we've spoken. I was worried out of my head. I went by your mother's house. She told me she'd spoken with you, and you were in need of rent money. What's going on?"

"Stormi, it's been a long night. Let me take a shower and we can talk when I get out."

Justin walked into the bathroom and turned on the shower. When he closed the door, I ran to the phone and called Gabby.

"Hola, Gabby."

"Hola, Stormi, what's up?"

"Gabby, I need your help. I need money. I'm not sure how much, but it will probably be a lot. Be prepared to come to Florida. I need you here to have my back. Justin's in trouble and I need back up."

"Stormi, are you shitting me?"

"Gabby, I'm serious."

Gabby starts to speak in Spanish, forgetting I only knew a few words.

"Speak English, Gabby."

"Stormi, how am I going to do that? I don't know anything about booking tickets."

"Have YaYa take you to do it."

"No, she won't do it. She'll ask too many questions.

"Then pay your crazy ass mother to do it."

"Your right, she'll do it. How much money do you need?"

"I'm not sure yet. Give me until tomorrow morning. I'll tell you exactly how much."

"Mantenerse a salvo mi amigo." (*Stay safe, my friend.*)

"Adios, Gabby."

Stormi Rain: Girl, you're not thinking straight. Reconsider your plan. It's obvious your boy Justin is book smart, but not street smart. Cut your losses and move on.

I heard the water from the shower turn off. I knew Justin would be walking out the bathroom any minute. I sat on the bed waiting for him. He walked in with a towel wrapped around his waist. Water was still running down his body.

"Stormi, are you hungry?"

I couldn't believe he had the nerve to ask me if I was hungry. I gave him that "you can't be serious" look.

"No, I'm not hungry."

Stormi Rain: Stop playing with this dude and ask him what's going on with the merchandise he has in here.

"Justin, we need to talk."

"Stormi, I'm hungry. I don't want to talk."

Justin gently pushed me to lie back on the bed. "Stormi, I feel so lost. I need to find my way back to you."

My heart started beating rapidly. I wasn't sure what he was talking about. He pulled my bottoms off and placed my legs on top of his shoulders.

"I want to show you that I need you."

Justin stood there staring at me. I could see the pain in his eyes.

"Baby, I've messed up big time and I need your help, but I don't want to talk about it right now."

I reached for him. I wanted to hold him in my arms and tell him it would be all right. I could see my man was broken. Tears started running down my face. Justin began kissing the inner parts of my thighs, and then I felt his tender lips on my labia. I became aroused; I could feel my sadness drifting away. He was taking me to another dimension.

I knew Justin was my soulmate. He was my motivation.

Justin pleasured me until I screamed, "enough."

He removed his towel and stood holding his pole of life. He walked over to the nightstand and opened the drawer. He pulled out a small glass vile that had white powder in it. He poured the powder onto my stomach. He got on his knees and used his letter "J" necklace to scoop up the powder and snorted it. That was the first time I noticed the end of the "J" was like a small spoon.

Stormi Rain: Get yo ass up. This dude is on some other shit. He's a dope head. Don't let him get you caught up.

Once he snorted all the powder off my stomach, things got intense.

Justin was working every part of my body. He was making me crazy, and I felt obliged to make him feel the same way. Before I could think about what was going to happen next, I was on top of him.

I let go of my inhibitions and turned into his seductress. My body was my weapon. I thrusted up and down slowly on the tip of his pole of life, teasing him with my wet jewel box. I held on to his strong shoulders while he sucked on my tits one at a time, intensifying my orgasm. The beads of sweat on his forehead were a sure sign that he was trying not to cum. I wanted to make him crazy, so I sped up my thrusting, bounced down, and took it whole. When I felt like he was about to give up his baby making juice, I jumped off. Justin leaned over for another vile of the white powder and took another snort. I got up, walked into the bathroom, and started my shower. I wanted to relax and take my tired ass to bed.

THEY CALL ME STORMI RAIN

20

IS THAT CRACK?

I woke up in the middle of the night extremely thirsty. I looked over at the clock—it was 4:00 a.m. I reached over to kiss Justin, but he wasn't in bed. I threw the covers back and went to find him. As I stood up, I could hear the smooth groove of Maze and Frankie Beverly's "Before I Let You Go" playing. That was my jam. I danced my way into the living room. Justin was nowhere to be found. I walked over to the stereo and saw Justin lying on the floor behind the bar with a glass pipe in his hand.

I thought he was asleep. I walked over, pushed him, and told him to get up, but Justin was unresponsive. I called his name several times and still no response. I got on my knees and bent down to see if I could feel him breathing. My nerves were so bad I couldn't tell if he was breathing. I rolled him onto his back. His face looked normal, but his lips were white and his eyes were closed.

I cried out to him. "Justin, please wake up."

I didn't know what to do. I kept shaking him, but he still didn't respond. I decided to tilt his head back and try to administer CPR. I didn't have any formal training, but I knew I needed to get some air into his lungs. I closed his nose, breathed into his mouth, and tried to do chest compressions. At first it didn't work, but I continued and he started breathing. He still didn't open his eyes. I knew I needed to call the paramedics, but I was scared. I didn't want them to see the stolen merchandise.

Call the paramedics and trust God. He has brought you through hard times. The Lord is on your side. Don't run. Stay and help Justin. No matter what's in the house, God will make it invisible to man. God is your peace in the midst of this storm.

I dialed 911 and told them my emergency.

Stormi Rain: Aww shit, we're in trouble now. They'll come in and see all this stolen property. Someone's going to jail, and it's going to be yo ass. Don't be stupid. Get your shit and leave.

Justin was determined to go to college and get his degree. If he were caught with stolen merchandise and drugs, he would lose his scholarship. I needed to help him, and help myself. We didn't need this to ruin our lives. I got a wet towel and cleaned Justin's face. I took the crack pipe and threw it in the trash. It took all the strength I had in my body to move those TVs into the hallway. I locked the door to the second bedroom where the shotguns and stolen jeans were.

I remembered my mother used olive oil as blessed oil. She would take the oil and rub it across my forehead as she prayed. I searched the kitchen cabinets until I found some. I held it up and asked God to bless and purify it in the name of Jesus. I unlocked the front door and sat on the floor beside Justin. I begged God to give him a second chance.

"Father God, you don't have to show me No Mercy, but please show some to Justin."

I took the oil and put it on my finger. I drew a cross on Justin's forehead and asked God to heal his body and renew his spirit. The paramedics rushed in and moved me out the way. They put an oxygen mask on Justin to get him to breathe nor-mally. Once they stabilized him, they transferred him onto a gurney and told me they'd be trans-porting him to Florida Presbyterian Hospital, and that I could meet them there.

I was a nervous wreck. One of the paramedics held my hand and told me not to worry. He said Justin was going to be all right. He was stable.

I looked up to heaven and said, "Thank you, Lord! I owe you one."

Once the paramedics left, I had to speak with the head firefighter. For some reason, they dis-patch the fire department along with the paramed-ics when you call 911. He wanted Justin's info, name, birthdate, and occupation. He wanted to know if he was a drug addict. I told him I was asleep and I woke up extremely thirsty. I heard music playing and I headed to the living room. I found Justin on the floor unconscious. I explained I didn't have any knowledge of him using drugs. I told them I'd contact his parents.

When everyone cleared out, I sat down to take a breather. I needed to think things through. I knew I needed to call his parents. But before I could do that, I needed to figure out how I was going to remove the stolen property from his apartment. I didn't want his parents to come here and see what Justin had resorted to. I called Trent. As soon as I heard his voice, I broke down. I cried until I got tired. Trent was begging me to calm down. He wanted me to tell him what was wrong. He could hear the fear in my voice. Once I was able to speak with clarity, I told Trent what happened. He went straight into boss mode. He told me he'd be on the next flight out to come get me, and that he was sending someone to clean out the apartment. He told me to pack my bag and be ready to come home with him on the red-eye.

I called the hospital to check on Justin. I told them I was his wife. They said he was stable; he had a team of doctors working with him. The nurse said I could see him later in the evening.

When I got off the phone, I stretched out in the middle of the floor faced down. I began to cry out to God. My life had been full of tragedy, heartache, and pain. I set out to avenge all the wrongdoings to my brother and my best friend, and now the love of my life is in danger of losing his. I begged God to save him, and I asked Him for forgiveness of my sins.

"God, when will I have some peace?"

I laid on the floor in the fetal position, sobbing like a baby. The doorbell rang and I had to get up. I opened the door. There were five thugs standing in front of me. The guy in the front told me his name was Marko. I immediately slammed the door and locked it. I ran to the bedroom where the shotguns were and grabbed one. I could hear them beating on the door. I got on the floor and tried to get under the bed, but I was too big. My heart was beating out of my chest. I sat on the floor with the gun pointed upwards. I was trying to figure out how to load it with the shells I found on the floor. I pulled the pump down and heard something click. I pulled the trigger back and shot a hole in the wall. It scared the shit out of me. That's when I heard the front door being kicked in. I laid down on the floor waiting for them to find me. I was trembling. I knew my life was over, but I was prepared to shoot whoever came through the door. I could hear their footsteps getting closer. I stood up and pointed the gun at the door. Before I pulled the trigger, I heard someone say, "Stormi, everything's going to be okay. Trent sent us to take care of you."

I opened the door.

"My name's Marko, you can trust me. Trent will be here in the morning.

We're here to move the merchandise and take care of you."

THEY CALL ME STORMI RAIN

21

How Do I Say Goodbye?

I got into the hospital bed with Justin. I wanted him to feel my body next to his. I wanted him to know he wasn't alone. I laid my head next to his. I could feel our hearts beating in sync—two hearts beating as one. I had been at Justin's bedside for several hours, talking to him and praying for him, hoping he could hear me. I wanted to be there when he woke up. My mind drifted to when we first met. He was with my cousin, Brittany. I remembered thinking to myself, *look at this fine brown-skinned brother right here.*

He was charming and educated. I remember telling Brittany, "He's almost pretty!"

Justin motivated me to strive for the best. He taught me to dream big. He had faith in me. He changed my life and gave me hope. He made me want to stop hustling. Justin showed me that college was the key to success. Now he's a crackhead. How do I live with this reality? I felt as if I was somewhat responsible. Justin knew Trent because of me. I could have persuaded Justin not to deal. He wasn't from the streets, so he got sucked in. If I could've changed the hands of time, Justin and I would have never met. The life I lived before him was not of a regular teenager. I was a young girl that had grown up too fast. I saw Justin as my savior, and that was too much pressure for him. His life was planned out before he met me. Now he lies in a hospital bed, detoxing from a crack co-caine overdose. I loved Justin. I would've given anything for this not to have happened to him.

My mind started working overtime. All I could think about was getting him the best treatment money could buy. I knew if I stayed here with him, I could help him recover and things would go back to normal. While working through my plan in my head, I fell asleep.

I dreamt of Justin and I walking along the beach, barefoot in the sand, holding each other's hand. We stopped to gaze at the beautiful sunset and he kissed me on the cheek. I wanted to wet my feet so we walked closer to the water. As the waves washed away the sand, you could see our shad-ows. I looked down at my shadow and saw it wasn't a replica of me. How could this be possi-ble? I stood next to Justin, holding his hand. But someone else walked away with him in the sand. I cried out to him, but he didn't hear me. They stopped to get a drink, and that's when I whispered in his ear. I was letting him know that I was still near. He stood very still. He knew I was there. He began to look around, but I was nowhere to be found. My spirit was fading fast. That's when I realized my time with Justin was over. Some love affairs are only for a season. In order for him to live, our relationship had to die. How do I say goodbye?

When I woke up, I decided it was time for me to call Justin's parents. I explained to them what had happened. His mother was devastated. They had a thousand and one questions for me, but I wasn't in any position to answer them. I told them the same thing I told the firefighter. His parents said they'd be on the first flight out in the morning, and that they'd see me then.

The majority of the day had already slipped away. It was time for me to go. I was expecting Trent to arrive on the red-eye.

I had been by Justin's side for hours and he still hadn't woken up. I kissed him on his lips, picked up my bags, and walked out the door. I went to the nurse's station to let them know I was leaving. I wanted to give them my contact information, so they could call me and let me know how he was doing. I reached over for a pen to write a note and I saw a picture of someone's footprints in the sand. I dropped my bags and ran back to Justin's room. I stood in the doorway staring at him. I removed my engagement ring and put it on his chest.

"I will always love you."

THEY CALL ME STORMI RAIN

Two Years Later

22

This is My Life

While lying on my king-sized bed, the sun kissed my face. I got up and walked onto the balcony that overlooked my beautiful backyard. I had an over-sized pool—the water running down the rocks made everything feel serene.

I decided I was going to have a pool party. I invited all my family and friends over for a day of fun in the sun. I felt like celebrating, but I couldn't tell anyone why. I had to keep it a secret until I knew for sure everything would be okay.

The last two years had felt somewhat like a dream. God finally saw fit to shine his blessings on me. At twenty-one, I was living my dream. I lived in a big house. I had three cars, and I no longer had to hustle.

It all started when I returned home from Florida. I was trying not to spin out of control. Walking away from Justin rocked my world. His mother was constantly calling me, asking me to go back and be with him. Justin was having a hard time dealing with our break up. I was, too, but I knew he needed to finish what he had started. He wouldn't be able to with me in his life. Justin got clean and went back to school. He stayed clean for a year, but he fell off and started smoking again. His parents sent him to rehab. We stayed in contact through letters. After he had been in the program for six months, I started visiting him. Justin was doing very well. We both knew we needed to move on, but it was impossible for us to let go. Once Justin was released, we started meeting secretly once a month. Justin's mother saw us coming out of a motel room together, so she blamed me for his problems. She harassed me every chance she got. I became overwhelmed with guilt, and started going back to my counseling sessions with Doctor Montgomery.

I was making progress, but then my mother agreed to allow my father's bastard child to live with us. Everyone tried hard to keep him out of my way. One day he came into my room and asked if I was his sister. His sweet little face was so innocent. He wanted me to accept him, but my heart wouldn't let me. I grabbed all my belongings, put them in my car, and moved out that night.

As I was loading my clothes into my car, Reese happened to be driving down the street. She pulled over and asked what I was doing. She told me that she had a two-bedroom apartment and she needed a roommate, so I moved in that night. Reese and I mended our relationship and became good friends. Trent would come over and visit and we'd all have a good time. One day, while we were playing cards, he said he had an idea about how we could make a ton of money. He told us he'd pay all our bills if we allowed him to sell drugs out of our apartment. The complex we lived in was huge and it had the potential to make a lot of money. I wanted to take some time to think about it, but Reese was all in. I remembered Trent telling me that you should never conduct your business where you lay your head. Reese needed the extra money, so she was willing to do it. She begged me, and I finally gave in.

The business took off right away. The money they were making was incredible. All they had to do was sit back and let the customers' come to the apartment. Both Reese and I worked regular jobs.

Life was good. Trent would send someone over to handle the sales, and then he'd pay us for the use of the apartment.

I continued to go to therapy so I could keep my demons in check. Doctor Montgomery and I had become very close. She finally took the time to get to know me. I was no longer just a paycheck for her. We crossed the line of the doctor-patient relationship—we became friends.

Doctor Montgomery became fearful that she was losing her husband, so she asked me to monitor him. In return, she showed me how to invest my money.

Once I saw the returns, I convinced Trent to invest also.

Everything was going well until I came home one day to find Reese freebasing with one of Trent's workers. I didn't think anything of it the first time, but it continued until Reese became a full-blown crackhead. She lost her job and didn't have the money to take care of her addiction, so she became willing to do anything for the next hit. I walked in on Reese with two different men from the apartment complex. They were doing unmentionable things to her. I had a flashback; it reminded me of King raping Shannon. I got my gun out of my room, walked over to their butt naked asses, and put it to the head of one of the men. The other ran out the door. If that man hadn't begged me for his life, I would've been locked up for murder.

I called Trent screaming and yelling at the top of my lungs. I was having a full-on panic attack. Trent came over with his boys and moved me out. He found the men that misused Reese and his boys made them pay.

I asked Trent to get Reese some help, but he refused, saying, "What goes around, comes around."

Trent was still conducting business out of the apartment. Reese was able to stay because he continued to pay the bills. She became known for selling her body for drugs. Once I got myself situated, I went back for Reese. I took her to a well-known rehab center and paid for her stay. When I moved out of the apartment Reese and I shared, I moved into Trent's home.

We both knew we were meant to be. After all, Trent was the one consistent person in my life. He loved me to the moon and back. I loved him, but I still wasn't in love. I didn't even know if there was such a thing, but it didn't matter. We lived in his home for three months before we decided to move. Jessica wasn't pleased that we were together; she had a hard time giving Trent up. She refused to believe he didn't want her. Trent tried to continue working with her, but it became too complicated. She would show up in the middle of the night kicking the door, acting a fool. One day she called the house forty-five times in a row. We had to unplug the phone.

Trent met up with her to talk. I knew he still had a soft spot for her. After their meeting, Trent came home believing all was well. She told him she'd respect his decision to move on. He gave her some money to hold her over until she decided what she wanted to do with her life.

———— • ————

Three months later, Trent and I were sitting in bed eating dinner and watching TV. I heard a noise outside, coming from the balcony. I asked Trent to check it out, but he told me not to worry. He said it was probably a squirrel. The noise contin-ued. I couldn't relax, so I pushed Trent out of the bed with my feet and refused to let him back in. To appease me, he walked over to the sliding glass door and opened it.

He looked at me and said, "I told you, it was probably a squirrel. He's gone now, so can I please get back into the bed?"

Trent started to close the door, but Jessica's crazy ass popped up out of nowhere. She put her foot in the doorjamb to stop him from closing it. She scared the shit out of both of us. She hopped the gate to the backyard and climbed the tree to get to the balcony. She was cursing and banging on the door.

Trent opened the door and walked onto the balcony where she was. Jessica tried to claw his eyes out. He didn't want to hurt her, so he stood there holding her arms. My heart was beating fast. I couldn't believe what was happening. I got out of bed to look for Trent's gun. Trent and Jessica were wrestling on the balcony. Trent grabbed her and shook her hard until she pleaded with him to stop. He told her to leave. She begged him to let her come through the house, but he refused. She became enraged and started kicking the door, trying to break the glass. Trent grabbed her, pushed her against the railing, and told her if she didn't leave, he'd throw her crazy ass off the balcony. I gave the gun to Trent. He put it to her head and told that insane bitch to climb back down the way she came. Jessica begged me to let her come through the house.

There was no way I was going allow that bitch to walk through my house. I knew she wanted to get a hold of me.

I made sure she left the same way she came. She slid back down the tree. Before she left, she broke out all the windows in the kitchen and the windows in Trent's truck. That night, Trent and I made the decision to move and start fresh.

Now we live in a gated community.

As I sat thinking about the past, I didn't hear Trent calling my name. He was downstairs. I got up and walked to the stairs so I could hear what he was saying.

"Baby girl, how many people are you expecting? I'm on my way to the store."

"Get enough food for about thirty."

"Have you decided if you're going to tell your family about the great news?"

"I'm not sure if I'm ready."

"It's all up to you. Whatever you want to do is all right by me."

"I'll see how today goes, and then I'll decide."

"Okay, I'll be back in about an hour."

Trent left, and I started feeling nauseous. I lied down in hopes that my stomach would feel better. The phone rang as soon as I dozed off. I picked up and heard a recording.

"This is a collect call from Babette Smith, an inmate at a California correctional institution. To

accept the call, press one. To deny the call, press two or hang up."

I'm wondering how this backyard dog got my number. What could she possibly want with me? I decided to accept the call.

"Hello, is Trent available?"

"Why do you want to speak to Trent?"

"Ma'am, no disrespect, but I really need to speak with Trent. It's a life or death situation."

"Babette, stop with the bullshit. How did you get my number, and what the hell do you want with Trent? How do you even know him?"

"Who am I speaking with?"

"Stop playing games. You know it's me, Stormi."

"Oh my God, is it really you? How's my son doing?"

"If you wanted to know about your son, you should've called my dad. Why are you calling my house?"

"Stormi, I know you hate me, but please don't hang up. Not until you hear what I have to say."

I wanted to hang up, but I was curious. I needed to find out how she knew Trent.

"Babette, you have ten minutes."

"Stormi, I know you're not going to believe this. I confessed to a crime I didn't commit. You see, I'm bipolar, and I had been off my meds for months when I showed up at your family's house. I'd been having an affair with your father for a couple years, and out of that union, we had a child. When your father refused to leave your mother for me, I went off my meds and went into a very depressive state. I had suicidal tendencies. That night I showed up at your parents' house, I was totally out of control. I needed your father to take his son because I was no longer able to take care of him. Before I could ring the doorbell, a young man walked up and asked if I needed help. I don't remember what my response was. I'm sure it was something that didn't make sense. While I was standing in front of your house, a man named Trent drove up and asked me to come to his car. He wanted to know why I was standing outside your house. I told him my story. He told me he could help.

He said the only way I could get my son to live with his father was if I shot Derrick and went to jail. He gave me a gun. I was out of my mind at the time. I would've done anything. When I started taking my meds again, I remembered what I'd done. I tried to tell the police my story, but I'd already been sentenced. The police refused to re-open the case. There was an Officer Jenkins—I think she believed my story because a few weeks later I got a visit from Trent. Trent promised me he'd hire a high-powered attorney and have the case reopened. All he wanted me to do was keep his name out of it. He told me because I'm men-tally ill, the attorney could file an appeal. That was a couple years ago. I haven't heard from him since. I decided to just let it go and focus on doing my time, but then I met his girlfriend, Jessica. She had been arrested for drug trafficking. We were in the dayroom and she was running her mouth about how she was put out of her mansion by a girl named Stormi. Well, we both know Stormi is a unique name. I started hanging out with her. She told me her story, including how her trafficking of drugs was taking care of you. She hates you, and she's still in love with Trent. She continued to work for him. He has hired an attorney to help with her case. I convinced her to give me Trent's information, in case something happened to her in jail. Stormi, I know I've caused you a lot of pain, but if you could find it in your heart to help me, I would be forever grateful."

Stormi Rain: Hang up the phone and pack your bags. You're sleeping with the enemy.

I heard enough, so I hung up the phone. I refused to go into panic mode. I had too much at stake. There are two sides to every story, and I was determined to find out the truth. Things were just starting to look up for me. Trent and I had been together through thick and thin. I couldn't imagine turning on him now. I didn't want to walk away from my new life, but I wouldn't live with someone who tried to have my brother murdered.

"Baby girl, I'm back. Come see if I got everything you wanted."

Trent was home and I had to make a choice. I could say nothing and we could go on with our day, or I could trust him and let him tell me what happened. I walked down the stairs to meet Trent in the kitchen. I stood there staring; praying that what Babette told me wasn't true. I needed Trent. What we had together was a good thing.

"Baby girl, what's wrong? You seem out of it."

"I received a disturbing phone call and I'm not sure how to handle it."

"From who? Is everything okay?"

"No, Trent, everything ain't okay. The call was from Babette."

"Who's that?"

"You know who she is. She's the mother of my little bastard brother."

"What did she want?"

"I think you already know. You look nervous and you're starting to pace. You want to tell me what's going on? Because she gave me an earful."

Trent got on his knees, grabbed me by my waist, and held me tight. "Baby girl, I want you to know I love you with all my heart and soul. Everything I've done was for you."

"What are you talking about, Trent?"

"I was tired of seeing you suffer at the hands of others. So, I just got rid of some people that caused you pain. You had already been committed twice, and I didn't want that to happen again. I vowed to make you happy."

"What did you do, Trent? Tell me."

"Baby girl, just tell me one thing. Do you love me? Will you ride for me like you did for Justin?"

"What are you talking about, Trent?"

"You remember when Justin was in trouble and you told me you was his ride or die chick?

"Yes, Trent, I remember. I will ride or die for you, but only if you haven't betrayed me."

"Okay, here it goes. I had my boys get King and Reese hooked on the pipe. When you told me that King raped Shannon, and she tried to kill herself and eventually succeeded, it bothered me. I saw first-hand what her death did to you. I had my boys supply King with crack cocaine and he got hooked, just like I knew he would. Once they stopped supplying him, he had to find a way to feed his habit. That's when he robbed a store. He's now in prison, being someone's bitch. Reese was never your friend. She only pretended to be. Even after you settled your differences and moved in together, she wasn't your friend. Reese got a hold of your social security number and applied for credit cards in your name. She tried to sell the cards on the street. My boy came across one and brought it to me. He didn't recognize the name on the card because no one knew you as Simone. I fixed your credit and took care of Reese. I made sure the pipe was her new best friend. I didn't think you'd spend your money on paying for her rehab.

That dude Juan, Gabby's mother's boyfriend, I threw him to the wolves. Raping a little girl is foul play, and the consequences are severe. Rape and be raped. He's now living in Mexico in a wheelchair."

I wanted to look into Trent's eyes when I asked him my next two questions. So I had him stand up and look at me.

"Trent, did you turnout Justin too?"

"I introduced him to the hustle, not the product. He did that to himself. But, I did have his supply cut off. He was in too deep."

"This is my last question. Did you shoot Derrick?"

"No, I didn't shoot Derrick, but I did provide the gun."

"What the hell do you mean, you provided the gun?"

"I was there when that crazy bitch and her son were standing outside your house. I drove up and asked her to come to my car. I could tell something was wrong with her. She rambled on and on about how her son deserved to live in his father's house. I told her I could help her make that happen. I gave her my spare gun and told her to shoot it in the air and wait for the police to arrive. I told her they'd take her to jail for firing a gun in public. She was supposed to spend maybe a month in jail. While she was gone, her son's father would get custody. I figured she was lying about the boy being your father's son. I knew if she got arrested, she'd go away. I did that for your mother. That crazy bitch saw Derrick coming up the street and she shot him in the stomach. That shit blew my mind. I drove off. She still had my gun, but it was untraceable."

"I can't believe you put a gun in that crazy bitch's hands. You almost cost Derrick his life. Yeah, your story sounds believable. But I remember Justin telling me that you told him that Derrick had inherited my debt. What about that?"

"Stormi, I wanted you from the very first time I saw you. I've always loved you. When you came to me to settle your debt, you asked me to watch over Derrick. I told you I would. You walked out of my life and into the arms of another man. I was crushed. That same day, I saw Justin getting out of his car at your house. I knew he was on his way to see you. I got jealous. I drove up and told him to tell you that Derrick had inherited your debt. I did it to be spiteful. You know I'd never hurt Derrick."

I didn't know whose story to believe, but I wanted to believe Trent's. I was so overwhelmed I decided to call off my celebration. My nightmare had just begun.

THEY CALL ME STORMI RAIN

23

The Price of Sin

I finally had everything I wanted. The possibility of losing it all made me feel sick to my stomach. My life would change drastically if I allowed the information I just received to affect me. I had to think long and hard about what to do; it wasn't just about me anymore. I had stopped taking my anxiety medication a couple of months back, and had been coping with my panic attacks on my own. I learned to take deep breaths and relax when I felt overwhelmed. It worked for the most part, and when it didn't, Trent would be there to pull me through.

After he told me his side of the story, we sat on the couch and cried together. He told me he loved me and he never meant to hurt me. All he wanted was to make me happy. I was inclined to believe Trent. I couldn't imagine him hurting Derrick. He made everyone pay for all the hurt and pain they caused me. I will be forever grateful. Babette can rot in hell. I needed some quiet time. I walked upstairs to our bedroom and got in the bed. I had to deal with my mental demons. I left Trent in his office having a drink. I just wanted to go to sleep. I tossed and turned, but I couldn't get my mind to settle down.

I thought about how hard it had been for me. My life had been a rollercoaster ride and it appeared as if I'd never get off. I heard Trent coming up the stairs. He was intoxicated.

"Baby girl, I was coming to check on you. Do you need anything?"

"I was trying to sleep, but I'm too wired up. My mind is all over the place."

"Listen to me, overthinking can put your body into stress mode. You have to remain calm, Stormi. Trust me, I'd never hurt you. You're the love of my life."

"My stomach is hurting. I have to go to the bathroom."

"Okay, I'll go downstairs and get you some ginger ale. That should settle your stomach."

"Thank you."

Trent went downstairs as I got out of bed. I could feel something running down my leg. I ran into the bathroom and sat on the toilet. I couldn't believe that I had started peeing on myself. Trent came into the bathroom with the ginger ale.

"Are you all right? There's blood on the bed and drops of blood on the floor. I didn't think you were still supposed to have a period."

"I'm not! I must be spotting. I read it's normal to spot in your early months. My stomach is hurting, though."

"Drink this, it should help."

"Put it on the nightstand. I don't want to drink while I'm on the toilet."

"Okay."

Trent walked out of the bathroom and I began having severe pain in my back and stomach. I was cramping and constipated. I kept bearing down, trying to relieve myself. I was moaning because I was in so much pain.

"Baby girl, you okay in there?"

"Yes, it's just taking forever for me to shit. My back is killing me."

"Just take your time. Don't strain yourself. If you keep pushing that hard, you might push out the wrong thing."

"Boy, shut up."

I sat on the toilet for another twenty minutes and finally I could feel it coming out. I was pushing as hard as I could. I knew I might end up with hemorrhoids, but I didn't care. I just wanted some relief. Finally it hit the water, but it felt like it came out the wrong part of my body. I got up off the toilet and looked in the water. I stood there staring. I wanted to scream, but sound wouldn't escape me.

Trent walked into the bathroom and looked at me. There was blood all over the floor. I stood there in shock. I was bleeding profusely. He grabbed a towel, reached into the toilet, and pulled out our baby girl. I stood there watching him trying to get her to breathe. I remembered singing "Jesus Loves the Little Children."

Stormi Rain: Death is the termination of one's life. Some die of old age, some die from disease, others from suicide, homicide, or accidents. It doesn't matter if you die peacefully in your sleep, or a horrible death. The results are the same. You are one dead motherfucka!

As I stood there watching Trent hold my darling daughter, thoughts of my birth crossed my mind. My mother sat on the toilet in pain, believing she was relieving herself. Unaware she was about to give birth to me, she continued to push, thinking that I was some shit. Death stood by and waited for my tiny body to hit the water. As I slid down my mother's birth canal, the Holy Spirit unctioned my mother to reach down and save me before my newly-crowned head hit the water. God had mercy on her and allowed her first-born daughter to live. Well, he wasn't so gracious to me. There was No Mercy for me.

Stormi Rain: The heavenly places you once believed in—the sun, the stars, the moon, and the rain—all of God's heavenly creations, are just a figment of your imagination. Your soul ties to your creator have been severed. Continue to walk on the dark side of life. Revenge, wickedness, and maliciousness are your newfound friends.

THEY CALL ME STORMI RAIN

24

I Can't Stand the Rain

I couldn't stand the sound of rain hitting the hospital windowpane. It was dark and gloomy outside. My titties were engorged with breast milk and no baby to feed. They told me I had a miscarriage. The nurse had come in to give me a pill that would dry up my breast milk, but I refused. I wanted to feel the pain of not having my baby. I could hear the other mother's in their rooms bonding with their newborns while I waited for a social worker to come talk to me about taking care of the body.

I refused to allow my loved ones to visit me. I just wanted to be alone. I knew they were expecting me to go off the deep end. But I didn't. Not this time. I was stronger and I was wiser. I was tired of getting beat up by life. I decided to take control and move forward. Trent had been waiting in the lobby to see me. I had no desire to see him, or anyone for that matter. My priority was to get my little angel laid to rest. I didn't need any help to do that. While I waited for the social worker to arrive, I picked up the Bible that one of the nurses left on my tray. I opened it to 2 Samuel 11:1-2. This was the story of David and Bathsheba. I found it interesting that Bathsheba became pregnant by David while she was married to someone else, and even more interesting to know that her baby died. The story was just getting good when the social worker walked in. We talked for about an hour. She was sympathetic. Once all the paper-work was completed, she got up to leave.

She turned around and said, "I'm sorry, I forgot to have you sign the birth certificate. What do you plan on naming your daughter?"

I looked at her with a smile on my face.

"I decided to name her Justine, after her father, Justin."

THEY CALL ME STORMI RAIN

*"Now I lay me down to sleep, I pray the Lord
my soul to keep."*

The storm is quiet, but just for a season.

The storm will return.

COMING SOON:

Book Three in the *They Call Me Stormi* Series